I0586634

Books by Marilyn Ludwig

The Ghost of a Tree Remembered

Marilyn Ludwig

Book cover and interior designed by Ellie Searl, Publishista®
Cover portrait approved by Dana Scott
Map in public domain

ISBN-10: 0996742255
ISBN-13: 9780996742252
LCCN: 2017911722

ZAFA PUBLISHING
Downers Grove, Illinois

For members, past and present, of Junior Thespian Troupe 88284
Herrick Middle School, Downers Grove, Illinois

For Lois Sterba and the Downers Grove Historical Society
Thank you for keeping the history of our village alive and well preserved.

And for Nancy

"The past is never dead. It's not even past."—*William Faulkner*

Downers Grove

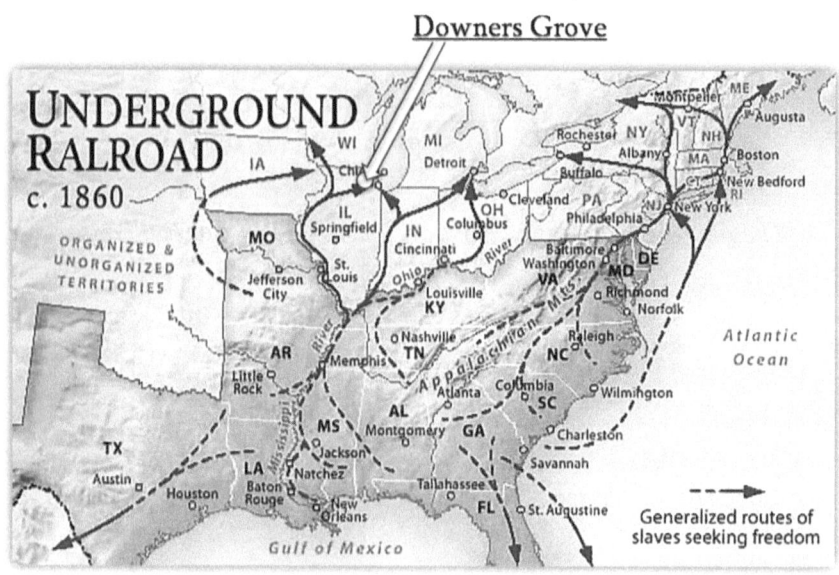

UNDERGROUND
RALROAD
c. 1860

ORGANIZED &
UNORGANIZED
TERRITORIES

IA

WI

Chi

IL
Springfield

MO

St.
Louis

Jefferson
City

MI

Detroit

IN
Cincinnati

Columbus

OH

Cleveland

PA

Rochester NY

Albany

Buffalo

Philadelphia

NJ

New York

ME

Montpelier

VT

NH

MA

Augusta

Boston

New Bedford

RI

Ohio

Louisville
KY

Washington

Baltimore

VA

MD

DE

Richmond

Norfolk

Nashville

TN

Memphis

AR

Little
Rock

Atlanta

AL

Montgomery

MS

Jackson

Columbia

SC

Raleigh

NC

Wilmington

Charleston

Atlantic
Ocean

TX

Austin

Houston

LA

Baton
Rouge

Natchez

New
Orleans

GA

Tallahassee

FL

Savannah

St. Augustine

Gulf of Mexico

Generalized routes of
slaves seeking freedom

Late October 2016

"Mrs. Lester, I am so sorry I'm late. The alarm didn't go off. I overslept. Mom is working, so I couldn't get a ride. I rushed here as fast as I could, but I still need to change."

Panting, out of breath, Kim knew actors were to arrive a half hour early, all dressed and ready to go—not still wearing pajama bottoms and a tee shirt. Miss Porter, the new teacher, glared in disgust, but Mrs. Lester nodded, giving her a sweet, understanding smile.

"Take a deep breath, Kim," Mrs. Lester said. "Happens to all of us. Here's a key to a changing room in the pavilion. Not the public restroom. Go through the passageway and take the door to the left. You can just see it from here. Hurry now. Visitors will arrive soon. And Kim, this is important. No matter what, you must return the key immediately when you return. To me—not to anyone else. Do you understand?" She waited for Kim's puzzled nod. "Good. Never remove the chain from around your neck. Leave it on; it's long enough. You'll still be able to open the door. Once inside, keep the key with you at all times, around your neck, hidden under your clothes. Understand?"

Kim nodded again. Mrs. Lester was way too serious, but Kim was relieved to still be allowed to take part in the Living Cemetery event. And thank goodness Miss Porter hadn't taken over Drama Club yet. Farewell to becoming a Junior Thespian this year if she had. She took the key—an old-fashioned one that didn't look as if it would fit any lock she had ever seen.

Covered with fancy designs and scrolls, hanging on a simple gold chain, it resembled jewelry found in antique stores. A very old key that looked, well, almost magical. "I'll return it immediately. Thank you so much, Mrs. Lester!"

The two teachers watched Kim rush toward the pavilion. Ann Porter shook her head. "After being completely unprepared at our final rehearsal yesterday and now late for the actual event, I'm surprised you're allowing her to participate. And she's supposed to portray Leah Faul? Several girls wanted that part."

"She'll do fine, Ann. Wait and see. I expect she'll be the best of the lot."

Claire had been teaching too long, Ann thought, aware that she would run a much tighter ship. Until now, she had felt sorry for Claire Lester, with her husband dead, no children, and about to leave—even before the end of the semester. Perhaps the school board had been wise to encourage her to take early retirement. This business about the key was most peculiar. Any second she expected Kim to return saying it didn't work.

"That key didn't look like the one the historical society gave you for the restrooms," she said.

"You mean, this one?" Laughing, Claire Lester held up an ordinary modern key. "No indeed."

"But where did you get the one you gave Kim? Who gave you it to you?"

"I wish I knew," Claire said. "Or perhaps I don't; I haven't decided. The truth is, I have no idea who it was. Five years ago, the first time Drama Club took part in Living Cemetery, an elderly woman in period dress came up to me. I thought she was one of the adult players, although her costume was more authentic than the others. She looked very much like the old photos I've seen of Mrs. Blodgett, the early settler who lived in our historical museum. Anyway, she handed me the key and told me to use it for latecomers. Then she pointed out the door it would fit. I would have returned it, but I never saw her again. I have learned to trust that key implicitly. Wait and see, Ann. Just wait and see."

Chapter One

━━━

Five Years Earlier

"THANKS, MRS. LESTER." LIZ HAVELKA grabbed the odd key and raced to the pavilion. That certainly had gone better than she expected, although she didn't think she'd ever seen her theater teacher so flustered— at least not unless it was during a first dress rehearsal and things were in their usual mess. She guessed this Living Cemetery gig meant a lot to Mrs. Lester. Liz supposed it was an honor for Drama Club to have been invited by the Downers Grove Historical Society to take part in what was meant to be an adult affair—until they couldn't get enough volunteers. Dressed in period costumes, all of the eighth-grade members and a few promising seventh graders would portray many of the important people buried there. The more modern ones died in the 1930s, but the others died of disease or were killed during the Civil War, coming home in boxes mainly from Tennessee. It was a small cemetery right on Main Street—much too old to be in the least bit creepy. No ghosts ever hung out—not even on Halloween night.

But Mrs. Lester was certainly acting strange this morning. Not just dramatic, as she often did, but really weird. She had had two keys, one in each hand—this curiously old-fashioned one and another that resembled anyone's house key. Liz would have thought the latter was the correct one, but after a long pause, Mrs. Lester had given her the unusual one. From around her neck, Liz removed the long chain holding her precious locket. She would add this key to the chain. It would never do to lose it after all the trouble that was still waiting for her once she stood next to her assigned tombstone. She wondered if it were possible to receive minus Thespian points. Well, if anybody could, it was Liz.

She had been assigned the role of Martha Blanchard Carpenter but was completely clueless about the woman. Instead of practicing her part, she had gone to a sleepover, where she spent most of the night plotting with her best friend Dannisha and a few others how she might get Nicky to invite her to the Halloween dance. They had almost convinced her to do the asking herself, if all else failed. At least she had talked the girls into dying her hair pink, although not until Liz had spent hours giving Danni almost authentic African braids. Danni looked gorgeous, Liz thought, with a headful of little braids all threaded with different beads and ribbons. Liz wished her own fine hair could accommodate such a style. "No, I'd look ridiculous. I'll just have to be pretty in pink," she'd told Danni.

Come to think of it, why hadn't Mrs. Lester said anything about her pink hair? She was always saying, "Never change anything about your appearance without asking the director first." The theater teacher must have been really rattled not to notice, or else she knew the bonnet would cover it.

Liz's information sheet about long-departed Mrs. Carpenter was still in the pocket of the cloak, in her gym bag, right where it had been since she had been given the costume. Maybe she could glance at the notes just once while she was changing. Then she would put her trust in Thespis, the god of theater, to keep her from letting Mrs. Lester, Drama Club, and the historical society down. But she didn't regret the sleepover. It had been the break she needed from hearing Mom whine about Dad leaving once again. If only they'd get a divorce like many of her friends' parents had. It wouldn't be pleasant, but at least it would be over. At times, Liz thought she no longer cared what her parents did. She wanted to live her own life for a change.

Now for the key. How was it supposed to fit into the lock on the door Mrs. Lester mentioned? They were not the same shape at all. Perhaps it would fit another door? No, none of the locks on the three doors looked right.

"Liz, wait up!"

"Nicky?" Was he going to ask her to the dance now, when there was no time?

"Wait for me! Don't open the door yet." Out of breath, Nicky Aubrey also held a bag containing his costume. "Mrs. Lester said to catch up with you 'cause you have the key."

"Well, all right. But if there's only one changing room, I get to go first." Without removing the chain, she showed him the key. "I can't figure out how to work it, though. It doesn't fit." She held it up to the lock, barely touching it, and the door creaked open.

"Nicky?" Where was he? He must have gone first. How rude! Dropping the chain under her shirt, she stepped inside. "Nicky, where are you?"

Before she even had the chance to change, she was outside again, and the building had vanished. No building, no Nicky, and no anything that was familiar.

"Nicky, where are you?" Silence. "Okay, guys, if this is a joke, it's a good one. Nicky? Dannisha . . . Danni?" No answer. Not that she really thought it could be a prank. She was alone on a strange road covered with boards, surrounded on both sides by lots of trees—mainly oaks and maples. No friends portraying early settlers at the cemetery across the way. There was no across the way, and no cemetery. The clothes she wore weren't her own and weren't her assigned costume, either. She was in costume all right, but an authentic one, rather than Goodwill/Halloween Happenings combinations. Instead of the short, simple hairstyle she had always worn, long sausage curls like she was in a Gone with the Wind movie hung past her shoulders. Her natural color was back—ordinary, mousey brown—not the pink creation that had been hers only a few minutes ago.

She examined the brown dress and cloak. They may have been more authentic but not something she would have chosen. Liz loathed brown, and all that material in the dress and petticoats was certain to make her look fat.

"Could I have fallen and don't remember?" she whispered. In books and movies that sometimes happened. A concussion, loss of memory, strange things . . . She felt as if time had shifted; it didn't seem like morning—more like late afternoon. Or maybe this was all a nightmare, and she was still at the sleepover. She tried pinching herself, but it only hurt and didn't change anything.

Her gym bag was gone. What about her key and locket? Both Mrs. Lester and Dannisha would kill her if she lost them. Danni had given her the locket for her birthday. Both of their photos were inside. She felt around her neck. Thank goodness! The key and Best Friends locket were still there. She dropped the chain under her clothes again, close to her heart. If she still had the key and locket, everything would be all right—eventually—she hoped. Liz sat on a fallen log by the side of the road. She would wait. For what, she didn't know.

"There you are! Oh, you must have been so worried." To Liz's relief, a girl came rushing toward her. One she had never seen before, but at least she was no longer alone.

"Hi," she said, bewildered. The girl was dressed in a similar fashion, so saying "Hi" suddenly seemed wrong. "Hello," she tried again.

The girl laughed. "You must wonder who I am. I'm Leah, and I've come to take you to the Carpenters' house. I'm truly sorry I'm late, but the stagecoach driver should never have left you alone. I will report him to Papa and Mr. Carpenter."

"That's okay . . . I mean, all right," Liz said softly. She hadn't been on a stagecoach, had she? "I don't want to get anyone in trouble. But where am I? I don't understand."

"I don't wonder, dropped off like a load of hay. You're on Plank Road."

Plank Road? Memories of third grade social studies flooded back. Ogden Avenue used to be called the Old Plank Road. That explained the boards; they were planks. But this seemed more like a path than her town's busiest street. Well, whether this was a dream or a concussion, she had gone back in time, and there was nothing to do but accept it—for now.

"We had better hurry," the strange girl said. "We've a long walk ahead of us if we're to arrive by nightfall. I don't know about you, but I'm afraid of timber wolves. And I imagine you're hungry."

Timber wolves? Liz didn't know if the jittery feeling in her stomach was caused by hunger or the mention of wolves, or . . . just everything, even the time of day. She had been right that it was no longer morning. Perhaps she was hungry.

"Supper will be waiting, and Mrs. Carpenter insists upon punctuality for meals. Martha June is simply pining to meet you. We've been expecting your arrival any day but weren't given details. Then a farmer spotted a girl waiting alone by the side of the road. We didn't know if it was you, of course, but I volunteered to come find out. All I knew was that a girl would be staying with the Carpenters because her father, an old friend of Mr. Carpenter's, had entered the fight for the Union and was worried about her safety staying in Virginia. We don't even know your first name—just your last name, Gray."

Leah certainly chattered a lot. Perhaps she was nervous, too. Liz needed to respond somehow. "My name is . . . Elizabeth," Liz replied finally. Well, that was true, but Havelka, her Czech last name, seemed too different in this strange place. Until she figured out what was happening, Gray would work out fine. After all, Grayson had been Mom's name before she married Dad, and she had threatened many times to take it back again. "I'm Elizabeth Gray."

"And I'm Leah Faul."

Leah Faul. Liz knew that name. A lot of the girls wanted to portray her because she had died when she was only eighteen, and they wouldn't have to pretend to be old. At the cemetery, perhaps at this very moment, almost one hundred and fifty years later while Amy was pretending to be Leah Faul, Liz was meeting the real one. Amy didn't look anything like Leah, and her costume wasn't even close to being accurate. Good thing Leah didn't know when she was going to die. Liz would not be the one to tell her!

"Oh, there's your satchel." Leah picked up a bag that practically matched the ugly brown dress but was made of carpet. Liz had never seen it before.

There was no choice. As impossible as it all was, Liz followed Leah into the unknown.

Nothing looked familiar for miles and miles. Surely the distance between Ogden Avenue to downtown Downers Grove, if there had been a downtown back then, wasn't this far. Liz had walked it many times. But the tall prairie grasses and stretches of woods made the way seem an eternity. Autumn was in full swing, maple trees scarlet and gold. Liz wanted to stop and rest—and sleep, not just because she hadn't slept a wink at the sleepover—but Leah didn't sound like she was joking when she mentioned wolves. "How much farther?" Liz asked.

"Oh, you poor thing. After such a long, difficult railroad journey, you must be completely tuckered out. Then riding that uncomfortable stagecoach from Chicago, only to be abandoned. Did you think you were in the wilderness? This must be so different from what you're accustomed."

You aren't kidding, Liz thought, but said only, "Yes, it is different from back home."

"We'll be there soon. You'll like the Carpenters. They live in a fine modern house on Maple Avenue, close enough so you can walk to school, church, and shops. And a part of their house actually is a shop, a general store and post office. You don't even go outside to mail a letter. I hope I can live closer to town someday. School is a good distance from our farm. I may have to quit going. I don't always feel well, and it's hard for me in inclement weather. This is Union Street. We'll arrive soon."

Union. That was an earlier name for Main Street, not that it looked like any street Liz knew, and if it had later become Main, it didn't seem to be in quite the right place.

"Here we are." Leah dashed up the wide front steps of a white clapboard house with green trim and a small covered front porch. Liz thought the house seemed familiar, although not as fancy as the one she remembered. Without knocking, Leah opened the door. "She's the right girl, Aunt Martha. I found her." Then she turned to Liz. "You'll be fine now, Elizabeth. I must hurry home before I catch the dickens. I was supposed to help Mother with supper."

"Thank you," Liz managed to say. "Is Martha Carpenter your aunt?"

"Heavens no. But my parents are good friends, so I just call her that."

To Liz's relief, Leah waited until a middle-aged woman joined them in the front hall. "Aunt Martha, this is Elizabeth Gray. Must rush now.

Goodbye, Elizabeth. I hope to see you at school tomorrow, if Papa is able to give me a ride."

And Leah was gone, leaving Liz bewildered, not certain what to do next. School tomorrow? Back home, tomorrow was Sunday. Here it was nighttime, but she had no idea what day it was, much less what year.

Weariness and fright kept her from being an ideal dinner guest, which might have been fortunate. Mr. Henry Carpenter kept asking questions about her trip and what conditions were like at home, and Martha June, who seemed about her age or a little older, went on and on about all the wonderful things they would do together, but Liz thought she sounded phony, as if she weren't really pleased to have this new person in the house. Liz tried to show some appreciation for their hospitality, as well as enthusiasm for the meal, but her head started nodding and her eyes grew heavy.

"Oh, you poor lamb," Mrs. Carpenter said. "Henry and Martha June, hush now, she's almost dead in her tracks. Come, dearie, let's get you to your room, where Maudie will undress you. Ring for her, Martha June."

I can undress myself, Liz wanted to say, but she was too weary to speak or, possibly, to undress, so she just allowed Mrs. Carpenter to guide her up the steep stairs to a cold attic bedroom that seemed intended for her.

"Here's Maudie now. Maudie, you are to assist Miss Elizabeth prepare for bed. She is too tired to do it herself. Then return to the kitchen and help Cook with the dishes. Without even waiting for Maudie's answering curtsey, Mrs. Carpenter left the room, leaving Liz to gasp in amazement.

"Danni? What are you doing here?"

The girl who looked like Dannisha laughed. "Danny? Do ah 'pear to be a boy, Miz Lizbeth? Ah'm Maudie."

"Oh. Oh, I'm sorry. For a minute, I thought . . . It's just . . . You look exactly like Dannisha, my best friend back home."

Maudie laughed again. "Your bes friend a colored girl? With such a fancy name? Ah declare, Miz Lizbeth, that's hardly likely."

"But . . ." But what was there to say? This girl, with her hair wrapped in a scarf and wearing a long striped dress and dirty apron, wasn't Danni, any more than she was Elizabeth Gray. "Perhaps you and I will be friends, too, Maudie. You don't need to help me undress, though. I'd rather do it myself."

"Ah do as white folks sez, Miz Lizbeth. Ah'm a runaway. The Carpenters keep me 'cuz of the pure goodness of their hearts."

A runaway slave? It seemed to Liz that Maudie was an unappreciated, probably unpaid servant, and that goodness didn't have much to do with it. "Maybe if you help me unpack . . ." she said, not having a clue what was in the satchel she had been carrying.

Maudie opened it and pulled out the Living Cemetery costume. She shook her head in wonder. "Sech strange material. Ah never seen the likes of this afore."

"Oh!" Liz stood quickly and thrust the clothing back into the satchel. "That's special. I won't be wearing it here. It's just for back home." She felt for the chain around her neck. Yes, it was still there. Her locket, the key, and Mrs. Lester's costume were all she had from her own time. They were her only assurances that she would return.

Chapter Two

"ELIZABETH, DO WAKE UP! I let you sleep longer than I should. We'll be late for school."

"But it's the weekend. Wait . . . What day is it?"

"It's Tuesday, of course. I know it must be difficult when you arrived so late yesterday, but Mother thinks it's best to begin as you mean to proceed."

Not a dream then. Or if it was, she was still asleep. She struggled to remember the girl's name. "Martha?"

"That's right. Martha June. Oh, do get up and dressed. Maudie said you didn't bring any suitable clothes, but you're smaller than I am, so you should be all right. She hung some of my outgrown dresses in the closet. Hurry now, or your porridge will be cold. I'll meet you downstairs."

Martha June left the room, thank goodness. Reluctantly, Liz pulled back the quilt and stared at the flannel nightdress she was wearing. She had no memory of where it had come from or even undressing. It frightened her, not remembering. She wanted to wash her face and use a toilet. Did they have an inside bathroom? Nothing to do, she supposed, but to open the closet and see what was there. A plain blue cotton dress with long sleeves looked as if it might be suitable. No shoes, though. She'd wear the same boots that were magically on her feet when she arrived. She gazed into a small mirror over the vanity. It was still her face, even though her hair and everything else was different. Fortunately, her hair wasn't messy, but she had no idea how she was to recreate such a style. Perhaps this dream—nightmare—wouldn't last much longer.

In the meantime, the satchel . . . Where was it? No one must see her costume, although she wasn't sure why. Finally, she located it way in the back of the closet where Maudie must have put it. Good. Perhaps it wasn't smart to trust Maudie just because she looked like Danni, but she did anyway. She had also liked Leah but wasn't certain yet about Martha June.

A timid knock on the door. "Yes?" Liz responded, and the door opened. "Oh, Maudie, I was just thinking about you. Is there a bathroom in the house?"

"Oh, yes, Miz Lizbeth. Very modern 'un."

Modern, was it? Somewhat gross but at least it wasn't an outhouse. She was grateful she didn't have to clean it. Afterwards, she followed Maudie to the dining room. Once there, Maudie seemed to become a different person. She put on a starched apron and became the cook's helper. Liz sat next to Martha June and tackled porridge covered with brown sugar, not exactly her usual quick Pop Tart and small glass of orange juice.

"Coffee, Miz Lizbeth?"

"Coffee? Me?" Well, maybe a pumpkin spiced mocha latte at Starbucks. "No thank you, Maudie. I don't drink coffee. Shouldn't you be getting ready for school, too?"

Maudie gasped. "Oh, no, Miz Lizbeth." Mrs. Carpenter and Martha June stared at Liz. Apparently, she had said something terribly wrong.

"Go into the kitchen now, Maudie, and tend to the dishes. I'm finished, and you may take my bowl. I'll have another cup of coffee later."

"Yes, Miz Carpenter."

As soon as Maudie was out of hearing, Mrs. Carpenter turned to Liz. "Elizabeth, we must be discreet about Maudie's presence here—for her protection as well as ours. Perhaps someday she'll be able to attend school, but not here at this time."

"Why not?" Liz wanted to ask, but that seemed rude. Instead, she gave Mrs. Carpenter a questioning look.

"Maudie is a fugitive slave," Mrs. Carpenter explained. "She came up through the Underground Railroad, but she is truly too young to go on alone. She's staying here with us, in hopes that her father will join her soon and that the two of them will continue on to safety in Canada."

"I've heard of the Underground Railroad," Liz said. Well, she had—in elementary school social studies classes. Her Girl Scout troop had visited Graue Mill, one of the many stations in the area.

"I guess everyone has," Martha June chimed in. "Even in Virginia."

"We can't be too careful," Mrs. Carpenter said. "It's illegal to harbor slaves, and vigilantes after bounties for capturing and returning them are everywhere. We are breaking the law and would wind up in trouble, too. Don't even talk about Maudie in school. We must always be diligent about protecting her. Right, girls?"

Martha June nodded. "Yes, Mama."

"I won't say anything to anyone," Liz said. "It would be horrible if anything bad happened to her." But she caught the odd expression on Martha June's face. She looked almost guilty. Had Martha June told someone about Maudie already?

"Make haste, girls," Mrs. Carpenter said. "It wouldn't do to be late. Mr. Richards is not one to abide tardiness."

Martha June stood quickly. "That's for certain. Come on, Elizabeth."

Liz hoped she would recognize something on her way but nothing was familiar. "What's your school like?" she asked. "I'm in the eighth grade back home."

Martha June laughed. "We don't pay much attention to grades here. I'm not sure which one I'm in. I'm sixteen, so I might not remain much longer. Well, the school is on the same street as our house—Maple Avenue—but it's pretty far away."

Maple Avenue? Liz shook her head. Yeah, sure it was . . .

Martha June continued talking about the school. "We're all in one room, and Mr. Richards divides us up for reading and arithmetic. The children aren't well behaved, even though Mr. Richards is strict. He canes some of the boys daily."

"You're kidding! That's illegal!"

"Oh, you are a funny one. It must be very different in Virginia."

"I guess it is." When was she going to wake up? This couldn't be real. Liz supposed that for the present she'd have to pretend it was. Did Martha June want her here? Liz wished she could figure out if she liked her. She didn't give out the same positive vibes Maudie and Leah did. Maybe if she shortened her name Liz might warm up to her. Marty would be cute, but she seemed to prefer being called by her first and middle name. Liz might suggest a nickname once she got to know her better, but please God, let me be out of here before then. If only she could skip school and be with Maudie while she was here, although it would be nice to see Leah again. "Will Leah Faul be at school today?"

"That depends on whether or not her father can bring her over. She lives too far away to walk, and sometimes the horse is needed."

Right. They didn't have cars or buses back then. "I wish I could have waited another day or so before starting school."

"Feeling shy?"

Liz nodded.

"Well, you needn't be," Martha June said. "Probably no one will pay much attention to you because there might be a new boy in class. He's come to work at the Webster farm—all the way from New York City!" Martha June said New York as if she were referring to the Holy Land or maybe even Hollywood.

"That's good," Liz said. "I'd just like to blend in, if possible." She wondered what the school would be like but warned herself not to expect much. Just think *Little House on the Prairie* or *Tom Sawyer*, she told herself. Long benches, slates, blackboard, and chalk. At least the work shouldn't be difficult.

"You'll have to borrow some of my supplies until you're able to acquire your own," Martha June said. "I don't think there will be time for you to make your ink or carve a pen until Saturday. Of course we're not allowed to on Sunday."

Make ink? Carve a pen? She didn't expect laptops, but this was ridiculous.

About fifteen boys and girls of various sizes and ages stood outside a wooden building that looked more like a condemned barn than a school. "They're waiting for the teacher to ring the bell," Martha June said. "Be glad we're not late. Even girls get hit on the wrist for tardiness."

The girls and a few of the boys, gathered around another boy, seemed to be bombarding him with questions. Liz figured he must be the new student, the one who would help take attention away from her. Then Mr. Richards opened the door and began ringing a large bell. "Enter now in an orderly fashion," he commanded. "Absolutely no talking."

The group, disregarding the teacher's orders, entered the school in the rowdiest way possible, leaving the boy all alone. Liz stared at him, and he stared back. "Nicky," she whispered.

"Come on, Elizabeth," Martha June urged. "You, too," she said to the boy.

"Now, who are you?" Mr. Richards thundered. "I don't know how I can possibly accommodate more pupils." Liz had never felt less welcome by any adult, much less a teacher.

A boy wearing no shoes chimed in. "This is Nicholas Arnold, one of the workers who will help Pa on the farm. He's come all the way from New York City."

"Oh, fancy," the teacher said. "Don't go putting on any airs with me, boy."

"No, sir," Nicky muttered, looking down at his shoes. At least he was wearing some.

"Find a place to sit, but if you don't behave yourself, out you go. You seem awfully high and mighty for the likes of us."

Nicky might have become Nicholas and be as out of place there as Liz, but she could not imagine the boy she knew standing for this, and she waited for the real Nicky to emerge.

He didn't disappoint her. "In that case, Mr. Richards, I'll be on my way. I don't believe in staying where I'm not wanted. See some of you later." He looked pointedly at Liz before bolting out the door.

The other students gasped, but Liz gave an inward smile. Good for you, Nicky, although for her sake she wished he had stayed. Somehow, she needed to find the Webster farm. Coming next was her turn to face Mr. Richards. Would she be as brave? That barefoot boy certainly hadn't been. At first, he looked as if he might follow Nicky, but hunching his shoulders, he took his place on a bench.

"And now, young lady, may we hope you are about to remove yourself from our presence, as well?"

"Mr. Richards," Martha June said. "This is Elizabeth Gray. She has come all the way from Virginia because her father is fighting for the Union and doesn't think she'll be safe remaining behind. Her mother died only last year, and she would have been left all alone in a dangerous place."

Mother died? Oh, no, how could that be? Wait, Martha June said last year, and she didn't mean Liz Havelka's mother, but Elizabeth Gray's, a girl who didn't even exist. Or did she?

The teacher sneered. "And your connection with the unfortunate Miss Gray?"

"Major Gray is a great friend of my father's," Martha June responded, "and it's important to my parents that Elizabeth's time with us be pleasant."

"Be seated," Mr. Richards said quietly.

Martha June led Liz to her bench. "Squeeze over," she instructed the other girls. "My father is the head of the school committee," she whispered to Liz. "He's Mr. Richards' boss. He'd fire him if the committee could find another teacher."

Liz liked Martha June better for standing up to his nastiness. She knew the Carpenters were an important family historically and supposed she was lucky to have landed with them. Evidently, Nicky had not been so lucky. She wondered where he was now. "What happened to that boy Nicholas?" she whispered back. "Where do you think he went."

"Shhh, we'll get into trouble. He probably went back to the Webster Farm."

By lunchtime, Liz almost wished she had followed Nicky. The lessons were tedious and meaningless to her and often shocking, particularly when the day had started with various students reading Bible verses (poorly) and everyone dropping to their knees to say The Lord's Prayer. Fortunately, she knew it from Sunday School. If she hadn't, she might have become acquainted with Mr. Richards' cane, in spite of being a girl with, supposedly, important family connections. Hadn't they ever heard of the separation of church and state? The Bill of Rights had been written back then. She guessed it didn't mean much to them. The lucky kids probably didn't have to take Constitution tests, though. That would face her back home later in the year—if she ever returned, of course.

Some of the class disappeared at lunchtime. "Their parents need them," Martha June explained. "But look, the boys are organizing a game of Snap the Whip. Come on, everyone will play."

Snap the Whip? Too much talk about whips and canes here. "I don't know how," she said. "Maybe I'll just watch this time."

"There's nothing to it, and it's so much fun." Then Martha June examined her more closely. "You're still tired, aren't you?" Liz nodded. "And maybe homesick?" Liz nodded again, grateful for the unexpected kindness. "Would you like me to stay with you?"

"No, you go ahead and play," Liz said. "I'd like to watch." She sat on a bench made of logs. "I'll be fine right here."

"Come on, Martha June," someone shouted. Martha June gave Liz an encouraging smile and dashed off to join them.

Liz watched the game in amazement. The last time she had recess was back in sixth grade when all that happened was the girls would gather in a cluster and giggle about boys or make catty remarks about other girls, and the boys would either play baseball or have fist fights. Ages, sizes, and gender didn't seem to matter that much here. The children who hadn't gone home held hands in a long line. Then they started to run, faster and faster. The first in line suddenly stopped and yanked sideways and laughed while those at the other end were thrown to the ground. Everyone laughed then, before getting up to start the whole procedure again. What was the point? Liz wondered.

"Hey, Liz, over here," came a stage whisper.

"Nicky?" Liz looked around but couldn't see him.

"Behind you. Just walk into the woods a bit. Don't let yourself be seen."

Liz gave a cautious glance, but the group was getting organized for another dumb game of Snap the Whip. As soon as she stepped into the woods, Nicky appeared cautiously from behind a tree.

"Nicky," she said. "This is too bizarre. What are we going to do?"

"Figure out a way to go home, I guess. Do you still have the key?"

She pulled the chain from her dress. "I'll keep it safe, don't worry. I was hoping I had a concussion or was still asleep, but since you're here, too . . ."

He nodded. "I thought the same thing, but it's not likely we'd have the same dream." He indicated the bag he was carrying. "I've still got my costume but don't know what to do with it. Liz, I can't go back to that farm. It's not safe."

Nicky explained that more boys were to follow soon by train and stagecoach to become apprenticed laborers. "Practically slaves, really. Tim's father is a drunk; that's why he doesn't have shoes. The old man sold them. I'm not sure how I ended up there, but if I stay, he'll confiscate everything I've got, even if it isn't much. And I'm so hungry."

"He let you go to school." Liz had a hard time believing anyone could be so cruel. Nicky might have misjudged the farmer.

"No, I sneaked out and followed Tim. Told him that I had to come, just for today. I hoped to find you here, or at least someone else to help me."

"I was luckier than you." Liz explained her present circumstances. "The Carpenters seem to be a nice family. I'm not sure I like Martha June, but she may turn out okay. She stuck up for me with that awful teacher. Mr. and Mrs. Carpenter seem to be kind. And Nicky, they've got a runaway slave staying with them, who looks exactly like Dannisha."

"That's weird."

"Her name is Maudie, and I'd like her for a friend, if she'll let me. She hid my costume in a closet."

"Maybe you can put mine with yours."

"Maybe, but I don't know how I can suddenly explain carrying your satchel." It didn't look like anything a girl would have.

"I'll think about it. Try to meet me here after school."

Again, Mr. Richards came out of the building with a large bell, which he proceeded to shake as if to let out his unexplainable rage.

"I'll try, Nicky. Gotta go. What are you going to do now?"

"Hunt around for where the pavilion and cemetery used to be, I guess."

"Don't get lost." Liz hurried to the end of the line.

The afternoon started off more promising. Spelling, which hadn't been a subject for Liz since fifth grade, turned out to be a spelling bee. She had almost won her school's competition last year, and a good friend of hers had made it all the way to Nationals. She found spelling bees both challenging and fun and determined to finally win one here. The whole class was stumped by the word, *clandestine*, which puzzled her because it was almost completely phonetic, except for that final *e*. The students looked as if they'd never heard the word before. "Clandestine. C-l-a-n-d-e-s-t-i-n-e. Clandestine," she said, winning her first spelling bee.

"Correct," Mr. Richards said grudgingly. The rest of the students applauded politely, but Liz thought they really meant it. Martha June especially looked happy for her. "And I suppose, Miss Virginia, you can also tell us what the word means."

He doesn't like me, Liz thought, but why? "It means secretive," she said quietly, realizing suddenly that the word hit too close to home.

After that, there was another recess. Liz wondered if Mr. Richards granted them just to give himself a break. He clearly didn't enjoyed teaching. On the school grounds, she looked around for Nicky but was unsuccessful. If he couldn't go back to the farm, where would he go? Yes, she was definitely the lucky one.

Or was she? A frightening thought occurred. Might there really be someone whose last name was Gray and was the daughter of Mr. Carpenter's friend? They had been expecting that girl. What if she actually arrived while Liz was there? Liz, who was, essentially, an imposter. Nicky, at least, was one of several workers without defined identities.

Another girl, Carrie, ran over and grabbed Liz's sleeve. "You must come and help us, Elizabeth."

Liz laughed. "I'll try, but I don't think I know your games." It would be a mistake to be rude. She might need all the friends she could get. The game this time was Fox and Geese. That one she remembered from way back in kindergarten and first grade.

As the afternoon progressed, it became apparent to everyone that the teacher had taken an unreasonable dislike of the new girl. The other children began to squirm in discomfort. It would have been different if they were the ones picking on a classmate. That was fair in their world. But he was being even meaner than usual—calling on her constantly, and then pouncing if she didn't respond immediately. Calling her Miss Virginia, rather than her name, seemed more than a little hostile.

"I'm telling Papa," Martha June whispered to her. "He is being terribly unjust."

"Don't worry about it, Martha June. I'll be fine."

"Miss Virginia, step to the front of the class right this instant. Since you feel you must whisper, perhaps you would be willing to share your great knowledge with all of us. Do tell us everything you know about our president. You folks down in Dixieland have heard of him, haven't you? The man who will squash you like boll weevils on one of your own cotton plantations?"

That does it. I'm going to let him have it, Liz decided. "Actually, Mr. Richards, while there are cotton plantations in Virginia, my family doesn't happen to own one. We are against slavery, and my father is fighting for the Union right this minute. In my family, we put our beliefs into action." Unlike you, was her implication. If he was so damned loyal to the Union and so against the South, what was he doing in this pokey little school? Why wasn't *he* fighting?

"Indeed. And since you are such a strong believer in holding our states together, why don't you tell us everything you know about our president, if you even know his name."

This was too easy. Last February in seventh grade, Liz had written a report on Lincoln that she delivered orally. She wondered if she might know more than the teacher, considering all that would happen in the months and years ahead. It was important, though, that she not sound like a know-it-all, tempting as it was.

"Abraham Lincoln was born on February 12, 1809, near Hodgenville, Kentucky," she began, pleased that she had a good memory for dates. "He had an older sister, but his little brother died when he was only a baby. Later, the Lincolns moved to a farm in Indiana. When Lincoln was young, his mother Nancy Hanks died, so his father married a woman named Sarah, who was very good to him. They moved to New Salem, Illinois." Thank you, Mrs. Lester, for helping me be so good at memorizing. I hope I get to thank you in person someday soon.

"Continue," Mr. Richards said, sounding completely bored.

"All right. I'll try. Abraham wasn't able to go to school much, but he taught himself a lot. When he got older, he decided to enter politics but instead fought in the . . ." she struggled for the name while the teacher looked impatient . . . "Black Hawk War! That's it! Then back in New Salem he was a shopkeeper and postmaster. Finally, he got into politics." How much longer did she have to go on? Richards wasn't even paying attention to her but was glancing through some papers. She stopped.

"I will inform you when you are through, Miss Virginia."

"Uh—okay. Later he studied law and started practicing it. He married Mary Todd and had two children but one of them died. It was very sad. Then he was elected to the U.S. Congress and went to Washington, D.C. When that was over, he gave a famous speech back in Illinois. He said, 'A house divided against itself cannot stand.' Abraham Lincoln hates slavery, and so do my father and I. That's why I'm here."

"Go on."

More students than one had fallen asleep, although some, like Martha June, were looking at her in admiration. "He had several famous debates with Stephen Douglas, but he didn't become a senator the way he wanted. He became the Republican nominee for president and was elected in 1861, right before the war started."

Oh, God, what year was it now? What shouldn't she know? She looked around wildly, her eyes finally landing on the blackboard, where he'd written, October 22, 1863. Thank goodness she hadn't mentioned the Gettysburg Address. That hadn't happened yet. "And he signed the Emancipation Proclamation on New Year's Day, January 1, 1863," she said triumphantly. She must stop before she made any mistakes. "That's all I know," she finished lamely.

"Are you quite sure?"

"Well, it would be smart for him to stay out of theaters," Liz muttered, quickly returning to the bench.

"That sounded most impertinent," the teacher said. "What did you mean?"

"Oh, nothing, really," Liz said. "I just got tired of talking."

Mr. Richards grabbed his cane. "Come here and hold out your hand." The rest of the class gasped.

"You're going to hit me? Why? What have I done?"

"Right now," he said.

Liz walked to the door instead. "No, Mr. Richards," she said calmly. "You may not hit me. No one is allowed to hit me. I'm a guest of the Carpenters and a visitor to this school. But I won't return." Shaking, fighting back tears, Liz fled from the building.

That might have been a dumb move, she thought, once outside, but what was she supposed to do? Allow herself to be struck? Back home, her mother would have called the police. "But I'm not home," she said. "That is, I am home, but it's all wrong." She walked over to the trees. "Nicky? Nicky, are you there?" No answer, and she wasn't sure she could find her way back to the Carpenters. She would wait until school was dismissed, whatever time that was. She wondered what Martha June would say. Never more alone, she sat on the log bench and burst out crying.

As it happened, she wasn't alone for long. As she learned later, after a few stunned moments, Martha June gathered her belongings, stood, and walked to the door. "I won't be returning either," she said. "I wonder what my papa will say about this. He considers Elizabeth's father a hero and a cherished friend. She did nothing to deserve your treatment of her." Martha June didn't stop to see Mr. Richards' reaction but knew she would hear about it from the others.

Outside, she found her guest in tears. "Elizabeth, don't cry. It will be all right. Mr. Richards was horrid. Wait until I tell Papa. He won't stand for this."

Liz sobbed. "I want to go home. He was so unfair. What did I do wrong?"

"Absolutely nothing. He's always been rude but never this bad. You did right to leave."

"You left, too. Won't you be in trouble?"

"Not me. I had almost decided school was a waste of time. You just helped me make up my mind. I'll work on sewing and cooking and reading at home. Maybe we can learn together."

Liz nodded through her tears.

"Elizabeth, I wasn't sure I wanted you to come here, but now I'm glad. Can we be friends?"

"I'd like that," Liz said.

Chapter Three

ON THE WAY HOME FROM school, Liz and Martha June encountered Leah Faul—and Nicky!

"Elizabeth," Leah greeted her. "It's good to see you again. Martha June, I was going to wait for you after school. You're out early."

"Yes," Martha June said. "Mr. Richards was dreadful to Elizabeth, and neither of us are going back. Wait until our fathers hear about it. Leah's father is also on the school committee, Elizabeth."

Nicky started. "He didn't hit you, did he . . . Elizabeth?"

Liz shook her head.

"No, but he would have," Martha June answered, "if she hadn't stood up to him and left."

"I'm probably not returning either," Leah said, "at least not while Mr. Richards is the teacher. But that's not why I needed to see you. I ran into Nicholas, here."

Nicky grinned. "She did run into me—literally. Crash!"

Leah ignored the humor. "Nicholas needs our help, Martha June." She explained the conditions Nick had encountered at the farm. "He can't go back there. Tell them what you overheard, Nicholas."

"Well, it wasn't clear at first, but I'm starting to put things together. It might not mean anything because Mr. Webster was drunk. I heard him say that soon he would be very rich because he knew where there was a runaway. I think he must have meant a slave."

Martha June gasped. "We must tell Papa immediately!"

"But what about Nicky—I mean, Nicholas? If it's not safe for him at the farm, where should he go? Your place, Leah?"

Leah shook her head. "I don't think I can ask. There are so many of us at home right now, even without our Martha."

"Leah's little sister died when she was only eight months old," Martha June explained. "She's buried in our new cemetery."

Leah blinked back a few tears. "Yes, she was the first one buried there."

Liz and Nicky stared at each other. The cemetery—exactly where they needed to go. "That is so sad, Leah," Liz said. "I'd like to pay my respects by putting flowers on her grave. Would you take me there sometime?"

"I'd like to go, too," Nicky said. Both of them tried to appear casual, but Martha June looked at them suspiciously.

"Let's get back to the problem at hand," she said. "What to do with Nicholas. We have a room in the barn that would be fairly comfortable until it gets too cold. We can ask Papa. I don't think he would be allowed to stay in the attic with Elizabeth and . . . and another guest there." Martha June suddenly seemed uncertain, worried.

That look again. Liz wondered. Had Martha June told someone about Maudie—maybe without meaning to? Martha June had been about to mention Maudie but caught herself in time. Liz would ask her about this in private later.

"Are you hungry, Nicholas?" Liz asked, changing the subject quickly.

"Very," he said.

"At least that's easily solved," Martha June said. "You'll come home and eat supper with us. Will you come too, Leah?"

"Yes, thank you. Your mother invited me. Father will fetch me later tonight after his meeting at the Hall."

Walking back, Liz learned that Leah was thirteen, the same age as she. At first, she had thought Leah was older—perhaps even older than Martha June, but after learning that Leah was one of ten children and had many responsibilities, Liz realized that's why she seemed so mature. Sometimes, Martha June seemed even younger than Liz. But Martha June had a much older brother, as well as two others who had died tragically, and had always been the baby of the family. Liz was an only child. She wondered how that might have affected her. She'd never thought about it before.

Home for supper, they learned to their dismay that Mr. Carpenter was leading the meeting at the Hall and would not be home until late that night. Fortunately, Mrs. Carpenter welcomed Nicky without a fuss. Maudie did not make an appearance, and Liz wondered if that was customary when a new person was in the house. They had made an exception for her because Major Gray was Mr. Carpenter's friend, and she would be living with them. Besides, she and Maudie were practically attic roommates.

Mrs. Carpenter bustled into the kitchen to help, and Martha June promised to be right along. "After we eat, Nicholas, I'll show you where you can sleep in the barn. We'll keep your staying there quiet until I talk to Papa. Then you must tell him what Mr. Webster said." Thankfully, Martha June followed her mother into the kitchen, leaving Liz and Nicky alone.

"Nice people," Nicky said.

"Yes, although I wasn't sure at first about Martha June. We do need help if we're going to get home."

"I don't think we can tell them the truth, though."

Liz nodded. "How could they believe it? I don't believe it."

"We need to see that cemetery."

"And hope like crazy it's the same one."

"It must be," Nicky said. "I remember seeing a baby's headstone."

"What about your costume? Should I put it with mine?"

"That would be a big help. I can't keep carrying it around."

Liz thought. "Keep your satchel, and just give me the costume. I'll dash upstairs with it. Won't take but a minute."

"Okay," Nicky said. "I'll go to the kitchen. Do you suppose boys helped out in those days?"

Liz had no idea and didn't waste time answering. Upstairs, she found Maudie in the room opposite hers, with the door open.

"Miz Lizbeth, more strange clothes? Where they come from?"

"Maudie, I can't tell you, but I need you to add them to mine. Will you trust me, please? They have nothing to do with you or with anyone here."

Maudie nodded, remaining silent.

Then, to Maudie's absolute shock, Liz gave her an enormous hug. "Thank you, Maudie. I think you'll be my best friend here. And not just because you remind me of Danni back home."

Maudie didn't respond to Liz's overwhelming overture of friendship, but she didn't seem displeased, either. She explained that she would not be going downstairs until the supper guests had gone. "Ah be safe right here," she said.

"I don't think you'd be in any danger," Liz said. "It's only Leah and, well, a friend of mine. But you know best. I should get back now. Please put these clothes in the closet. And remember, I'm trusting you, too."

Maudie agreed. Liz wondered if she had actually told her the truth. Was Nicky her friend? She hardly knew him. She thought he was cute and a terrific actor, and she had wanted him to invite her to the dance. Cute, acting, a possible date—it seemed so far away. Never mind the things she used to want. All Liz really wanted now was her mother.

"Oh, dear," Mrs. Carpenter said, when she heard about how both Nicholas and Elizabeth had been treated at school. "I can't imagine what Henry will say."

"Well, I can," said William, her older adopted son, who had joined them for supper. "He is going to be furious. He's certain to fire Mr. Richards now."

"Not unless he can find another teacher to take his place," Martha June said. "No matter, though. We're not going back there. Is that all right, Mother?"

"We'll see what your father says. But if you stay home, will you discipline yourselves to keep on learning?"

Martha June nodded. "I can teach Elizabeth, and she can teach me. She knows more than anyone in class, including Mr. Richards."

Liz doubted that, but it was pleasant to have Martha June approve of her.

The talking stopped then because there wasn't much more to say, and everyone was hungry.

After the dishes were cleared and washed—without Maudie's help—and Leah's father had arrived to take her home, Martha June told William about Nicholas's plight. William was concerned also by Mr. Webster's words about runaways.

"Probably just spirits talking," he said, "but we can't take a chance. No, Nicholas can't return there. Until we can work out something better for him, the room in the barn is a good option. I'll go down to the Hall and see if I can catch Dad at his URR meeting. He needs to know immediately what Nicholas overheard, although I'm sure he'll want to talk to him about it."

As soon as he left, Martha June explained the relationship. "I had another brother named William. He died quite young, so I never knew him." She stopped and sighed. "My brother, Walter, who was named after my uncle, died in a horrible explosion. The William you just met used to be named William Potter, but his family couldn't take care of him, so he became my parents' foster son. Later, they adopted him. Now he has the same name as my brother who died. He is really the one I'm closest to in the family, even though he is much older."

Awfully complicated, Liz thought. But what a lot of tragedy for one family.

"William is lucky," Nicky said.

Martha June nodded. "Yes, he is, and so am I. I'll take you to the barn now, Nicholas."

"Thank you. Look, would you mind calling me Nick? No one back home calls me Nicholas."

"Nick," Martha June agreed.

"And I'm Liz or Lizzie." She would like to shorten Martha June's name but didn't think she should suggest it—not yet. "I think I'll go upstairs to bed now. I'm still pretty tired from traveling. Goodnight." Maybe she could spend time getting to know Maudie.

Chapter four

LIZ DREAMED OF BLACK PAPER cats, orange tissue paper pumpkins, and an ear-blasting rock band. She wore a long, lacy purple gown and held a black and purple sequined half-mask on a stick. Her date was in complete Phantom of the Opera attire. Soon, he would pull off the white mask and she would know his identity, discovering who had brought her to the eighth grade Halloween dance. Then, as if on command, he reached up to his face, grabbed his mask, and . . .

"Miz Lizbeth, wake up. You be late."

"What?"

"It be time for church."

"Where am I? Danni?" The Halloween dance disappeared. She was still stuck in olden days Downers Grove, but even so, something else was wrong.

"Church? Maudie, how can it be Sunday when yesterday was Tuesday?"

Maudie giggled. "Laws, you is a strange 'un. Yesterday be Saturday, so today be Sunday. Git up, or I be the one to catch it."

"All right, Maudie." Liz would figure it out later.

Liz picked a black and gray dress, somewhat fancier than the others, hoping it was suitable for church. Downstairs, she found Mrs. Carpenter, Martha June, and Nicky already at the table. Nicky seemed as confused as she felt. He looked at her and shrugged. The others, though, acted as if Nicky being there was a natural, matter-of-fact occurrence. What had happened between the time Nicky went to the barn and now?

"Will Mr. Carpenter join us?" Liz asked. Other than her first night, she hadn't seen the supposedly close friend of her father's.

Mrs. Carpenter and Martha June looked at her strangely. "Of course not, Lizzie," Martha June said. "You know he won't be back before tomorrow."

Tomorrow. Which could be just about any day of the week, Liz thought. There was no way of telling.

Martha June told them that her father had donated the land to build the church but wasn't a member of the congregation. "He's not much of a church-goer," Martha June said. The small wood-framed building didn't look anything like the enormous Methodist Church on Maple Avenue in 2011, Liz thought. But Maple Avenue didn't look the same, either, although she thought that during the long, bewildering trek with Leah her first night here, she might have recognized the house that had been moved next to the historical museum a few years ago.

The church service was as grim as Liz had expected, but she found it far more pleasant and certainly less demanding than school had been. Men and boys were seated on one side, women and girls on the other. There didn't seem to be any Sunday School classes. She wasn't disappointed. Nothing was expected of her, except to stand, sit, sing, and listen. She liked the minister, especially when he preached about the evils of slavery.

Leah and her family were present. Leah whispered that they normally went to the Congregational Church, but Leah's father wanted to hear the Methodist minister's sermon. Liz wondered how she might approach the subject of the cemetery and, hopefully, ask Leah to take Nicky and her there after the service. But Mrs. Faul was frowning at their attempts to whisper, so she kept quiet. But she started to hope. With any luck, they would go home today. Wouldn't that be wonderful? And yet . . . She stopped. Would it? She thought about the history fact sheets she and the rest of Drama Club had received about many of these people. Mainly because the information was scanty and didn't really tell a story—just facts and a lot of dates—she hadn't studied them carefully.

She and Nicky had to return to the cemetery in order to go home. But if they left today, they'd never find out what happened to Maudie, or whether or not Mr. Webster was really trying to report runaway slaves. She would miss Maudie and Leah, who would only be alive for five more years— an unhappy fact she did remember reading. She might even miss Martha June. Still, whatever was going to happen would occur whether or not she and Nicky remained. They would not be able to make a difference. Yes, they needed to go home.

After the service, Leah shook her head when Liz and Nick asked about going to the cemetery. "I can't today. My mother needs me to take care of the younger children. She is coming down with a cold and must go to bed as soon as we get home."

Mrs. Carpenter would attend a meeting of the women's auxiliary, and Martha June planned to visit a sick friend. "I promised before I knew you were coming. I really must not disappoint her."

Hoping it was the truth, Liz and Nicky assured Martha June they would have no problem finding their way home. They would take a chance on getting lost, they decided privately, if it meant having the opportunity to figure things out alone.

"That was a stroke of luck," Nicky said. "They were too busy to pay much attention to us."

"But now what?" Liz asked.

"We'll try to find the cemetery ourselves. We know that a blacksmith shop is on the corner of Maple Avenue and our present Main Street, although their Union Street seems to be west of there. Let's go to the blacksmith's that's there now, and then walk north. We might be able to find it."

Liz nodded. Even though the 1863 shop looked much different from the building she was used to, Nick's plan seemed sensible. Whether or not they were about to leave for good was another matter. "What if we can go home right away, Nicky? Should we?"

"What do you mean?"

"I mean you haven't talked with Mr. Carpenter yet about what that farmer said about runaways. At least, I don't think you have. I'm so confused about time here. At any rate, we don't know what he knows or if you told him. Maybe we're here because we're supposed to do something and shouldn't go home until we do it."

"You're confusing me."

"I know," Liz confessed. "I'm confusing myself. I want to go home, but I'm worried about Maudie, too."

"First, let's see if we can find the cemetery."

Soon Liz and Nick discovered that it wasn't that easy. Determinedly, they trudged through wet, soggy marsh before coming to a partial clearing that might be the cemetery. A stone in the distance was their first clue. This place was a greatly abbreviated version of what they were used to, but there was little Martha Faul's gravestone. "Only eight months old. How sad," Liz said. There were other stones as well. It seemed odd seeing them so new. But the cemetery looked totally different. For one thing, a creek ran right through it, and the part they needed to get to was on the other side.

"It's too deep for us to walk across," Nicky said. "We'll have to figure out where it ends and walk around." He pointed in a vaguely southwesterly direction. "The pavilion must have been built over there somewhere."

"Maybe. It's hard to tell with so many trees blocking everything. Especially that one." She gazed admiringly at a majestic oak with leaves of the brightest gold. "I don't think our autumns are as grand as theirs."

"No, this is more like a New England fall. Liz, I hate to give up, but I'm freezing, and we're not wearing coats. As weird as it sounds, I think it might snow." The only clothes Nicky owned—other than the jacket, black jeans, and top hat, now in Liz's closet—were the trousers, shirt with suspenders, and cap that seemed to have been issued to him magically. At least, thanks to Martha June and Maudie, Liz had an entire wardrobe to choose from.

The wind had picked up, the sky grew darker—Nicky was right. "Let's go," she agreed. "And here's hoping we don't get lost." And that tomorrow is not Thursday or some other unlikely day.

Fortunately, they arrived back in time for Sunday dinner, roast chicken with all the trimmings. Even more fortunate, Mr. Carpenter had returned early. Unfortunately, Nicky's prediction of snow proved correct.

"Brrr, most unusual for October," Mr. Carpenter said, after he acknowledged Nicky's presence with little fuss. "I'm sure we can find warmer clothing for both Nicholas and Elizabeth."

"We're calling them Nick and Lizzie, Papa," Martha June said. "So much easier. I wonder if I should shorten my name, too?"

"That is something for you to consider later," Mrs. Carpenter said. "Let Papa say grace now, and then we'll eat the fine meal Cook has prepared."

They bowed their heads, including Liz, who was not accustomed to saying grace. She had to admit she wasn't even used to having a meal with a family. More the norm for the Havelkas were table trays in front of the TV or standing up in the kitchen glued to their cell phones, or just eating a sandwich while on the way to somewhere. Maybe they were missing out on something important, she and Mom. They loved each other, of course, but this was more of a family than hers. She had no idea what Nicky's family was like, but he seemed more comfortable here than she did.

"Gracious father," Mr. Carpenter began, "we thank you for our fine home and this sumptuous meal. We truly appreciate your blessings and wish that more of your people were able to partake of them. We will do our best to make that happen. Please heal our troubled land and bring our states together again. Help your dark people in their efforts to win the freedom that all of us should be guaranteed. Keep our Walter safe on the battlefield and our first son William and second son Walter safe with you and your Son. Amen."

"Amen," everyone said. Liz no longer felt like an outsider. She was part of this, and this was her *now*. She remembered her words to Nicky. Should they go home even if they could? Was there a reason they were here? Were they supposed to do something before they returned?

After dinner, Mr. Carpenter took Nicky into his study to question him about what he had overheard at the Webster farm. Later, Nicky told Liz about their conversation. "It could be very important," Mr. Carpenter had said, "or just the rants of a drunkard. Also, we'll need to figure out what to do with you, young fellow. It's certain you can't return there."

Liz assumed all of them would be needed to help with the clearing up in the kitchen, but not this time. Cook and Maudie would take care of it, Mrs. Carpenter explained. Elizabeth and Martha June were needed in the parlor to help with quilt making.

"We aren't usually allowed to do this on Sunday," Martha June told Liz, "but the quilts are important work. Abigail, Carrie, and Barbara are coming, too."

Quilts important? Why? Liz tried to remember what she had read about soldiers' needs during wars—blankets and socks, surely, but handmade quilts? Seemed a waste of time and energy. At least, thanks to costume mending for summer theater productions, she should be able to do her part.

Liz was still troubled by some of the conversation at the dinner table. Henry Carpenter was anxious to talk privately about her father and conditions back home in Virginia. Great, considering she didn't even know what her supposed father's name was. She nodded but managed to look mournful. Mrs. Carpenter exchanged glances with her husband, who quickly said, "You need more time to settle in first. Our talk will wait until you've adjusted."

Which would be never—if she could help it. Martha June had told her the family hadn't even known her first name or when exactly she was coming. "Sometime in October was all we were told."

What if, Liz fretted, what if the real Miss Gray arrived when she was still here? How could she explain that? Well, she couldn't. In some respects, Nicky was better off. No one knew his circumstances. He could just improvise. As the star of Drama Club's improv troupe, Nicky was good at that.

The quilt project was amazing, Liz decided. Once she learned about it, she was proud to help. The quilts were meant to guide runaway slaves. Each one carrying a coded message would eventually hang outside safe houses—maybe on porch bannisters or clotheslines. If a quilt had an X on it, the runaways had reached a halfway point. Flying geese on a quilt showed which direction to take. The quilt Liz and Abigail were piecing together had a bear's paw pattern that meant runaways should follow the direction of the bear tracks because they pointed to the easiest route over the mountains.

Mountains? No mountains around here. She wished she knew where this quilt would go. Black blocks or drinking gourds, symbolizing the Big Dipper, meant that the house was a safe place to stop and rest. A bright star, of course, stood for the North Star. Liz wasn't sure how it would all work but knew she had never been part of anything so important.

Martha June whispered that she had cautioned the girls against asking her too many questions. "I told them it still hurts for you to talk about your family."

Liz smiled sadly. "Thanks, you're right, it does." Actually, it did hurt a whole lot; just not the family Martha June meant.

The girls were very nice and in many ways didn't seem much different from those back home. Martha June brought up the subject of nicknames. "Elizabeth wants to be called Lizzie or Liz. Do you think my name should be shortened, too?"

Abigail, who seemed the most talkative of the group, said, "Well, her name is perfect for shortening: Eliza, Liz, Lizzie, Betty, or Beth. Other names aren't that simple. Like mine, for example."

"Back home, I have two friends named Abigail," Liz said. "We call one Gail, and the other one Abby."

"More like Gabby," Carrie said, and the rest of the girls laughed, including Abigail.

"I think I'll stick to my full name," she said.

"Back to me. Martha June is such a mouthful, although I don't think Mama or Papa will ever call me anything else. They'll continue to say Elizabeth, too."

Until they discover I'm an imposter and come up with other choice names, Liz thought. "Well, we could call you Marty. That's cute."

The other girls shuddered. "Then people would think my name was Martin—a boy. I wouldn't like that."

"Sometimes people call me Barbie," Barbara said. "I wish I could just change my name. I don't like it. It makes me think of barbarians."

"Barbie is a cute name," Liz said. "It makes me think of . . . well, a lovely, fashionable doll. But Martha June, what about MJ, your initials? That could be fun."

"MJ." Martha June considered. "Modern and unusual, don't you think? I like it, but I'll choose who I'll allow to call me that."

So MJ Carpenter it was. Liz was amazed by the almost instant transformation she saw in Martha June's personality. Not so old-fashioned and, strangely, more sophisticated.

By the time fathers arrived to take the girls home, one of the quilts was complete, and the other two would be soon. They agreed to meet the following Sunday.

Not a bad day. Liz yawned. "I hope Nicky is okay. I guess I'll see him tomorrow. I wonder what day that will be."

Chapter Five

"TELL ME, MAUDIE," LIZ ASKED the next morning. "What day is it?"

"Saturday, Miz Lizzie."

"Of course," Liz said. "Everyone knows the day after Sunday is Saturday."

Maudie burst into delighted giggles. "You are a caution, Miz Lizzie."

Liz sighed. That was her, all right—an absolute caution. She put on what she hoped was an everyday dress and decided to find out what Saturday meant in the Carpenter household.

Mr. and Mrs. Carpenter and Martha June had left early that morning—Mr. Carpenter to attend to some dry goods orders for the store and MJ and her mother to see about decorations for the dance. "What dance?" Liz asked Nick, the only one present at breakfast.

"Evidently, there's a barn dance tonight," he said, "and it looks like we're going. Just found out about it myself."

Because of the cook and Maudie going back and forth from the dining room to the kitchen, they didn't feel free to talk. "I'm supposed to work in the store this morning. What are your plans?"

"No idea," Liz said. She was surprised MJ hadn't asked her to help with decorations.

"Come to the store with me. We should talk."

Henry Carpenter's general store reminded Liz of ones she'd seen in old movies. Sacks of flour and sugar, penny candy, farm equipment, jackets, boots—just about everything one could think of. "Nicky, this is amazing!"

"Maybe you should call me Nick like everyone else does. They'll wonder why you have a special name for me. Besides, I think I prefer it."

"More grown up," Liz agreed. "Okay, we'll switch. Nick and Lizzie instead of Nicky and Liz. What do you do in the store?"

"Sell things, I guess. Mr. Carpenter showed me around yesterday afternoon after we talked. At least I think it was yesterday. I'm mixed up about days. Things seem kind of fuzzy. I remember hearing that he sold most of his business to a Mr. Thatcher, who now has a store in town. That one carries even more things, but this one is also a post office."

Liz nodded. "I know what you mean about time. It's crazy. We were with Drama Club on a Saturday morning, but the next day was Tuesday, and the day after that was Sunday. And now, today is Saturday. Have we been here more than a week and just don't remember most of the days?"

Nick shrugged. "Well, seeing that the whole thing is weird, I suppose it makes sense that it doesn't make sense. I feel like we're seeing pictures on Instagram. You know, just snapshots of people's lives. We are given one experience and then we move on to the next."

"Like school, church, and for me, quilt making."

"At least you know where you'll be in the morning. I went to sleep in the barn and woke up in a back room of the store, with all strange clothes and no memory of how I got there. I guess it's going to be my new room. At least it's warmer than the barn."

They stopped abruptly when a man with two small children entered.

"Hello," the man said. "Hank away?" He didn't wait for a reply. "I'd like five pounds of cornmeal, and the children may have one piece of candy each."

Fortunately, the cornmeal was in a five-pound bag ready to go, and the children were familiar with the process of selecting candy. "I'm new here," Nick admitted, "and not sure how much to charge you."

The man opened a large ledger, which turned out to be a credit book. "I'll just write my name and what I took. That's the way Hank handles most of his business. See you folks around." Taking his bag of cornmeal and herding his children, now holding chocolate whips, they left as quickly as they'd come.

Nick examined the credit book. "I wonder if Mr. Carpenter actually gets paid for anything. I know he's also a shoemaker. Maybe that's how he makes most of his money."

"I guess," Liz said. "He seems to be doing okay. Things are just different here."

"I'll say. I need to see some of the money. I have no idea what it looks like or what it's worth. Lizzie, some of the people who are on our money weren't born back then. I suppose we'll see Washington, Jefferson, and Hamilton."

"That's true. They probably didn't even have Lincoln pennies." Liz had never paid much attention to whose picture was on what money. It was money—good for spending. Her mother was saving some JFK and Susan B. Anthony coins and had some old silver dollars in her jewelry box.

"I'm supposed to work until noon today," Nick explained. "Then maybe we can go exploring again to see if we can get to the other side of the creek."

Liz agreed. "I'm starting to get nervous about staying. What if the real girl they expected shows up? All they knew was that her last name was Gray and that she would arrive some time in October. They assumed I was the right one because who else could I be? And October is almost over . . . I think."

Nick whistled. "I see what you mean. At least I'm able to invent my own cover story, even though no one seems to care. I just said that because my father is a soldier and my mother is sick and staying with a relative, they thought I should come out with other boys to work on a farm. I kept it vague, but for some reason Mr. Carpenter bought it. He seems to be the trusting type."

"I'm afraid of him."

"No need to be. He's very nice."

"But don't you see? He wants to talk about my father and what's going on back in Virginia. He thinks I know things. But the problem is Major Gray is his friend. If he starts questioning me, he'll find out fast I'm not telling the truth. I like him, too, but I plan to avoid him."

"Elizabeth, you look so much better today," Mrs. Carpenter said at lunchtime. "I am relieved. I was worried you might be coming down with influenza."

"At least you should be able to go to the dance tonight," MJ said, "but I wish you could have helped decorate the barn. That was so much fun."

Had she been sick? Liz couldn't remember. At least there was an explanation for why she had been excluded from the activities.

Mrs. Carpenter said that Lizzy could attend the dance provided she rested in the afternoon. Nick was free to do as he wished until Mr. Carpenter returned, although she wasn't sure when that would be. She had a headache and wished to lie down.

"But I wanted Lizzie to go to Gracie's with me," MJ protested. "We are making socks for Union soldiers."

At least someone was *sewing socks for soldiers* besides *Sister Susie*, although they were probably knitting instead of sewing. Liz was remembering the old tongue twister exercises they used as theater game warm-ups. And was *Peter Piper picking pecks of pickled peppers?* Maybe *Billy Button was buying buttered biscuits*, or *She was selling seashells by the* . . . Oh, stop being silly, she scolded herself. Martha June was waiting for her to say something.

"That's all right, MJ," Liz said. "I'll go with you another time. Your mother is right. I shouldn't take any chances. I certainly don't want to get influenza and put everyone at risk, as well as myself. I should rest this afternoon." She sounded formal and phony, but that's the way they talked here. She and Nick exchanged glances. They might be able to search for a way around the creek after all.

But it didn't turn out that way. For one thing, shortly after MJ left for her friend's house, it started to rain—a hard, bitter, freezing rain that belonged more to winter than fall. Then Mr. Carpenter burst into the shop, just as Liz and Nick had decided to put their trip on hold.

"Nicholas, I need your help!" he said, obviously upset.

"Sure thing, Mr. Carpenter. What's wrong?"

"The Websters' barn burned down last night, and Tim is missing."

Tim. That was the boy who had brought Nick to school—the one who was barefoot. "Do they think he was in the barn?" Liz cried.

Mr. Carpenter shook his head. "We don't know. Some people are sifting through the smoking debris now. Emma Webster told us. The old man is passed out on the sofa, drunk. But Tim's bed wasn't slept in, and Emma says some of his possessions are missing. She doesn't know if that means he took them and ran away or that her husband sold them."

"That's why he doesn't have shoes," Nick said. "What would you like me to do, Mr. Carpenter? I didn't get a chance to know Tim very well, but I liked him, and he took me to school, even though he wasn't supposed to."

Don't say anything else, Liz warned silently. Don't let him know the reason you went to school.

But Mr. Carpenter wasn't thinking about them. "We need to form a search party to comb the woods—especially since nightfall will come early in this weather. The wolves have been a problem lately." Liz must have reacted, for he added quickly, "Don't worry. I'll take my rifle."

Nick grabbed a warm jacket, one that was for sale in the shop. "I'm ready now," he said. "Anything else I should know?"

"I'm not certain," Mr. Carpenter said. "Last night, Tim told a farm hand that his father wasn't the only one who could earn money that way. He didn't explain what he meant, and the farmhand had no idea. I don't like it, though."

Liz didn't like it either. Something was nagging at her. Something she needed to remember. Perhaps if she didn't try too hard it would come to her.

Chapter Six

ONCE IN HER ROOM, LIZ didn't want to rest. She wasn't sick, but she was tired and a little afraid of falling asleep. If she did, who knew what day it would be when she awoke? If Maudie were upstairs, too, she might distract her. Yes, there she was in her small attic quarters reading the Bible. Liz wondered who might have taught Maudie to read. She didn't think slaves could.

"Maudie, I'm bored to tears. Please come keep me company. It's cold in my room, but not quite as bad as in here."

"Miz Lizzie, ah'm not much comp'ny, but ah be willin' to try."

Liz hoped Maudie would talk about herself and her family. Maybe if Maudie felt more comfortable around her . . . What could they do together?

"Maudie, I guess I'm going to a dance tonight. What do you think I should wear? Will you help me decide and get ready? Unless you think it might be cancelled because of the weather."

"Ah don't think so, Miz Lizzie. The Stanleys' barn be right down the street. Ah be glad to help. And, if'n you don't mind me saying so, your hair could use some fixin'."

"Oh, I know. I've been wondering what to do about it."

For the rest of the afternoon, she and Maudie had a delightful time. The runaway slave, forgetting their differences, allowed Liz to be a friend. After seeing the full, flouncy skirt and peasant blouse Maudie chose, Liz burst out laughing. "Thank goodness for my acting class. I've never been so out of character before, but at least I'm not being typecast."

"Offen ah don't understand you, Miz Lizzie."

Liz grinned. "I'll bet most of the time you don't, Maudie. Well, don't worry about it. What kind of dance is this anyway?"

"You never afore ben to a barn dance?"

"Not exactly."

"Ah'm surprised, Miz Lizzie. Back in Missouri, even us slaves had barn dances."

"It's a dance in a barn. I get that. But what kind of dancing?"

Maudie giggled. "Here, square dancin', a course."

Square dancing! "Oh, good. I can do that." She could, thanks to her old-fashioned loser of a PE teacher in sixth grade, who insisted on a square dancing unit. Perhaps she'd return to her elementary school and thank the teacher—if she ever got back, that is.

Liz and Maudie refreshed each other's memories and soon were whirling around the room, hysterical with laughter—until they were stopped by a shocked Martha June.

Flushed, out of breath, Liz said, "MJ, you're home."

"I certainly am. And it looks as if you're fully recovered from your illness. Maudie, Cook needs you downstairs. At once!" Maudie fled.

"You just turned her back into a slave again," Liz protested. "Why? I had her acting and feeling like a normal girl. She was happy for once."

"Someday she might be free," MJ said, "but she's still a colored."

"Why you . . ." Liz stopped. What words would be safe—both for her and Maudie? "We both had a good time, Martha June. I like her, and she's my friend." The look on Liz's face said clearly, but I'm no longer certain about you. Forget about the friendly MJ nickname.

Time to change the subject, though. "Have your father and Nick returned?"

Martha June shook her head. "I don't know anything about them," she said.

That's right. Martha June had left the house before Mr. Carpenter had sought Nick's help. Quickly, Liz explained.

"You mean, Tim might have burned to death in the fire?"

Liz nodded. "Yes, although Mr. Carpenter thinks it's more likely he ran away. He said something about if his father could get money that way, so could he." Liz stopped at the expression on Martha June's face. The same expression as before. Now she remembered.

"Martha June." Liz could tell she knew what losing her nickname meant. "Martha June, did you say anything to Tim Webster about Maudie being here? Please tell me you didn't."

She stammered. "I . . . I didn't mean to. It just slipped out. Do you think that Tim . . ."

"I don't know," Liz said, "but it's possible Tim told his father, which is why Nick heard Mr. Webster bragging about getting money. Or it might be the reason Tim thought he could get hold of some."

"What shall we do?"

"*You* must tell your parents. We can't take the chance that Maudie is still safe here."

"I don't think anything can be done tonight."

"And we're all going to the dance," Liz said. "Will no one be home?"

Martha June shook her head. "No, not even Cook. She has the night off."

"So if someone comes into the house, Maudie will be all alone. We can't let that happen. We must either stay here or take Maudie with us. Oh, I wish your father and Nick were home."

"Please don't tell Papa. He'll be so angry with me. And I really didn't mean to."

"Then you'd better come up with a plan, Martha June, and fast."

But she didn't have a plan. Instead, she burst into tears and dashed from the room.

Now what? Liz wanted to talk with Nick first, but if he didn't return in time, she needed to let Maudie know what had happened. After all, it concerned her more than anyone else. Then she could almost hear her mother speaking. "Slow down, Liz. You always jump into things, and you always think you're right. It's a mistake to hold people to a higher standard than you do yourself."

"Yes, Mom," Liz whispered. She and her mother had not been getting along lately, but she wished she were here right now. Or better still, she wished she were there.

Liz sat on the bed. Think things through, she told herself. Think before you act. First of all, she didn't know where Tim Webster was, or if he had ever said anything to his father about Maudie. He had seemed like a nice boy—certainly not someone who would turn in a runaway slave for money. Martha June did act awfully prejudiced, but these were different times. Liz couldn't expect her to see Maudie the way she did. Probably Martha June never had a friend of a different race. And there were plenty of prejudiced people in Liz's time, too, and even those who weren't didn't have the courage the abolitionists had.

As far as Martha June blabbing out of turn, Liz was a fine one to judge. Always spouting off whatever was on her mind was something she did all the time—especially to her own mother. Martha June must feel terrible. "I need to talk with her again before I do anything else." Reminding herself to remain calm and patient, she walked down a flight of stairs to the girl's bedroom.

"MJ," she called, while knocking on the door. "I'm sorry I made you cry. May I come in?"

"All right," said a sorrowful voice.

Martha June, sitting on her bed, hardly looked up when Liz entered. Liz sat, putting a tentative arm around her. "MJ, I'm sorry. I know you didn't mean to give Maudie away. Anyone can make a mistake. I do it all the time. And really, we don't know anything. Did you actually tell Tim that Maudie was a runaway?"

MJ shook her head. "No, I just said we had a colored girl helping our cook for a while. But no one else in town has, you see."

"Well, that doesn't sound so bad. He might not have even paid attention to you. We just don't know for sure. And we don't know where he is right now. But look at you! If you don't get ready, I'm going to look much better than you at the dance tonight."

"You look fine, except your hair is messy again. But I don't think I should go now," MJ said. "I should stay and protect Maudie."

"It might seem more suspicious if we don't go, but you're right to worry about her. Is there somewhere she could hide while we're gone? We don't need to tell her much. Just enough so she'll stay safe."

MJ gave Liz a quick hug, grateful to be understood. "Thank you, Lizzie. I really am terribly ashamed of myself. There is a hidden partition in the downstairs closet. We haven't used it for Maudie because we thought she was safe. Now, maybe because of me, she isn't."

Downstairs they heard male voices, Mr. Carpenter and Nick returning. It probably wouldn't be possible to talk to Nick before they left for the dance. Once there, perhaps they could find a few minutes to be alone. A small chuckle escaped her. "What?" MJ asked.

"Oh, nothing much. You make yourself beautiful now. I'll tell Maudie you want to see her, and then you can get her up to speed. Say that because no one will be in the house tonight, she should stay hidden. Maybe tell her there have been reports of revenue hunters in the area. That should do the trick—without scaring her to death."

"The way you talk sometimes, Lizzie. I declare, they certainly talk strangely in Virginia."

"I guess so." She needed to be more careful, but the more relaxed Liz became, the easier it was for her to be herself—her real self, not Elizabeth Gray. And she had laughed before because it suddenly occurred to her that a certain dream was about to come true, but with a twist. She was going to a dance with Nicky, just not the eighth grade Halloween dance where she hoped to wear a black and purple gown. But a square dance! In a barn! In 1863! And she was wearing a skirt that had more material in it than all of her dress clothes at home combined, and she still had her long sausage curls.

Chapter Seven

ALTHOUGH THE TEMPERATURE HAD PLUNGED, it was no longer raining. Fortunately, the barn was only a short walk down the street on Maple Avenue. MJ whispered to Liz that she was very fond of the Stanleys' grandson. "You might say he's my beau," she said.

Martha June had a boyfriend? Liz kept forgetting that MJ was sixteen, over two years older than she. "Will I meet him tonight?"

MJ looked sad and, for a brief moment, closer to her age. "No, he's away fighting in the war. I . . . please don't tell anyone, but when he returns we'll be married." She blushed slightly. "We came to an agreement before he left. Papa approves."

But will her boyfriend return? Once again, Liz wished she had studied the information sheets. She might have known the man's fate. "I won't tell anyone," she said. "What's his name?"

"Eugene Farrar," MJ whispered. "I hope you will meet him someday."

"I'd like that," Liz whispered back.

Nick, who had gone on ahead, came back. "I wondered what was keeping you. Come on. The decorations are totally cool, MJ. Just terrific!"

MJ seemed confused but smiled her thanks. Liz grinned. *Totally cool . . . Terrific . . .* She wasn't the only one having trouble staying in character.

"Oh, there's Carrie and Emma. I promised to help serve refreshments. I will see you both later." MJ rushed to catch up with her friends.

"Totally cool? Terrific? How about Wow? Or Far Out? Or Rad? Or . . ."

"Yeah, I know," Nick said. "I should be more careful."

"I'm having the same problem," Liz admitted. "Nick, MJ told me she has a boyfriend fighting in the war. I hope he comes back."

"He will. They'll get married next year."

Liz stared at him. "How do you know that?"

Nick sighed. "Because I did what you were supposed to do. I read all of the Carpenter information. You forget that back home I was supposed to be Mrs. Carpenter's brother, Judge Walter Blanchard, who was killed in the war. Actually, that's going to happen in November."

"So MJ lost two brothers and an uncle. That family has had too much death."

"Most of the families around here have. Well, we'd better get in there. You and me at a square dance. You do remember the Virginia Reel, don't you? After all, you're from Virginia."

"Oh, no! Well, if I don't remember, I'd better come up with an excuse. But first, Nick, what happened? Did you find Tim Webster?"

Nick shook his head. "Not a sign. We'll continue the search tomorrow morning."

"If it really becomes tomorrow morning," Liz said. "Okay, let's go."

Nick was right. The decorations were super terrific. If only they could take everything back to decorate the gym for the Halloween dance. But she could tell everyone what it looked like—if she remembered. That was a thought. Would she remember anything when she returned, or would it all be erased from her memory? For now, she wouldn't worry.

Let's see—other than the barn, they could duplicate many of the decorations. Haystacks and pumpkins, of course, and all those cornstalks and maybe the sheaves of wheat. Not the horse carriages, nor all the people playing their fiddles—and not the spirit. No, there was something here they could never copy. Back home, they would be playing parts—pretending to be old-fashioned, even though their dancing would be modern. Maybe she could talk her friends into a few square dances—to make it more authentic.

The one thing that would be the same was the ratio of girls and boys. Only here, the scarcity of men was because of the Civil War. Back home, it was because of . . . well, probably indifference or thinking it just wasn't cool.

Liz started to explain to a group of girls why she wasn't an expert at dancing the Virginia Reel—"Well, I haven't been to many square dances"—when she was rescued by an unexpected ally, Mr. Henry Carpenter.

"That's quite all right, Elizabeth." Then he explained to the others. "I know Elizabeth's father, and he can be very strict in some respects. After all, Elizabeth is only twelve." (This was news to Liz, who was almost fourteen.) He winked at her. "My guess is that she would be more at home with the bunch up there." And he pointed to the loft, where younger children were rough-housing and paying little attention to the dancers.

"That is the way it was," Liz said in relief. "But I'd rather stay down here and learn."

Soon, she was participating in many different kinds of square dances, the patient caller explaining each one to the entire group. Sometimes Liz danced with MJ and sometimes with Carrie and Emma. A few times her partner was Nick. That was the best. She was having fun, but something other than normal concerns, like going home, kept her from truly enjoying herself.

It wasn't fair that Maudie couldn't come. She knew how to square dance and would love this. Instead, she was holed up in some hidden closet so she wouldn't be captured and sent back into slavery. Or maybe even worse. Liz wondered what happened to runaways who were caught. She could end up looking like some of those people in photos Liz had seen in the cellar of Graue Mill—large welts on their arms and backs from whippings. She might be sexually abused or even murdered. Liz knew she couldn't return to her own time until she knew Maudie was safe.

Nick noticed her lost in thought. "Liz, what's wrong. Are you sick?"

"No, but maybe we can find a private place to talk."

The only possibility was outside, away from where a few young people were smoking rolled cigarettes and some men were drinking, perhaps too much. Under a maple tree a short walk away seemed safe. Light-spill from the barn caused the tree's leaves to glow as if each leaf were a small reddish golden lantern. There, Liz told Nick everything she knew about Maudie, what MJ had let slip, and her worries about Tim and his father.

"So she's all alone in the house, hiding away in a closet. Does she even know why?"

"No, MJ just told her that it would be safer because she had heard reports of revenue hunters in town and that being in the house alone could be dangerous."

"I don't like it," Nick said. "The Carpenters don't even have locks on their doors. No one in town does. It's hard to believe Tim Webster would turn in a runaway slave, but I don't really know him. I'm pretty sure his father would betray his own mother for a bottle of whiskey."

"What should we do?" Liz whispered. "I'm scared."

"We'll go back. Look, I'll tell Mrs. Carpenter that you're sick again—that you got over-heated and I'm taking you home. I saw her before we came out here. She is sitting with some women talking. You wait here. I'll be right back." Then he looked around at some of the men who were becoming rowdy. "No, you come with me. Just stand in the doorway and look miserable." He grinned. "You can do that, right? Improvise."

Mrs. Carpenter looked toward the doorway in concern, but one of the other women interrupted, asking for a recipe. So Mrs. Carpenter just nodded to Nick, gave a slight wave to Liz, and turned back to her friend. Nick escaped quickly.

They rushed back to the Carpenters'—possibly just in time, for there at the front door two men were forcibly knocking. Nick and Liz came up behind them. "May I help you?" Nick asked.

The men looked him over. "We're looking for the man of the house. We've heard a rumor that needs to be checked out."

"I'm sorry, but no one is home right now. If you want to talk to Mr. Carpenter, you'll need to go down that way." Nick pointed. "Everyone is there at a barn dance."

"You're sure no one is here?" one man asked suspiciously.

"Positive. We left early because the young lady isn't feeling well. I must take her inside." Nick stood waiting. He would not open the door while the men remained.

Finally, they shrugged. "Maybe we'll see about that barn dance." But then they walked off in the opposite direction from where Nick had pointed.

"Inside fast," Nick said.

Nervously, Nick told Liz to push a chair and table in front of the door while he dashed to the backdoor to do the same. Liz obeyed, before glancing worriedly out the window. No sign of the men. Of course, she didn't know if their goal had been to find Maudie, but she and Nick couldn't take a chance.

"We'll guard the doors until the Carpenters come back, and then we'll tell Mr. Carpenter everything," Nick said, once he returned.

"I sort of told MJ that I wouldn't."

"Sorry, you'll have to break your promise. Too serious."

"What about Maudie now?"

"Go check on her. I wish she didn't have to stay in a closet, but . . ."

"I'll think of something," Liz said. "How are you going to handle keeping guard until I return?"

"I'm more worried about the backdoor than the front, so I'll go there. After you see Maudie, come down to the kitchen. Just nerves, probably, but I might be hungry. I didn't eat anything at the dance, did you?"

Liz shook her head, but she wasn't hungry. Normally, nerves had the opposite effect on her. She couldn't eat when she was frightened. "I'll go see Maudie," she said.

At the spare room closet, Liz knocked softly. "Maudie, it's me, Lizzie. I'm opening the door."

Inside the closet, Liz found another door. For a moment, it felt like last year's play. Suddenly finding herself in Narnia, though, couldn't be any more peculiar than this. But no snow or trees or white witch greeted her on the other side. Instead, she found a small room containing an army cot, a thin blanket, and a pail, probably to be used as a toilet. Not comfortable, but not quite as horrible as she had expected.

"You be home early, Miz Lizzie. I 'spected Miz Carpenter or Miz Martha June be likely to fetch me."

"We were worried about you, Maudie. That's why Nick and I came back. And it's a good thing we did. We may have been just in time to keep two strange men from breaking into the house. Everyone else is still at the dance."

"Oh, my, Miz Lizzie. Ah ben wishin' to go sleep in mah own room, but ah'll stay right here."

"Or, you could switch places with me, or better yet with Martha June."

"Beg pardon, Miz Lizzie?"

"You could go into Martha June's room, put on one of her fancy nightgowns and caps. Then you could get into her bed and face the wall. If anyone were to break in, no one would suspect that a slave would have such a fancy bedroom."

"Oh, no! Miz Martha June be mad at me."

"I don't think that will happen. In fact, I think it's a good plan. Now you hustle into Martha June's bedroom and change while I dash upstairs to get your things to store in here. Then I'll get the clothes you're wearing now and bring them here, too."

Poor Maudie had never known anything but obeying white folks' orders. She hustled while Liz followed her own directions—trying to ignore her mother's voice coming from somewhere deep inside. "Was that really wise, Liz, or did you do it for revenge?"

I don't know, Mom. Maybe that was her reason for putting Maudie into the nice bedroom. Maybe she was still angry with MJ and wanted to get back.

Chapter Eight

BOTH LIZ AND NICK WERE weary by the time they heard knocking on the front door, followed by a loud, "Why is this door blocked? What is happening in there? Nicholas? Elizabeth?"

They dashed from the kitchen to the front door, opening it to an irate, confused Henry Carpenter, followed by his wife and daughter.

"We can explain, Mr. Carpenter," Nick said.

"Maudie was in danger," Liz added.

"Maudie, where is she?"

"She's all right, Mrs. Carpenter. Lizzie disguised her and put her into Martha June's room. She's asleep now."

"My room? My bed? Why did you do that?"

"Hush," Mr. Carpenter said. "First, do you think she is still in danger?"

"Probably not, now that you're here," Nick said. "But when we came home, two men were about to come inside." He and Liz didn't know for sure if that had been their intention, but it did seem likely. "We stopped them just in time. You don't have locks on your doors, so that's why we barricaded them."

Liz continued. "But we were afraid they would get in anyway and search until they discovered Maudie's attic bedroom, so I put most of her things into the closet hideaway. I was afraid they might think my room was hers, but I couldn't clear out everything." She could hardly say that the room she'd been given wasn't much better than Maudie's. That would sound ungrateful, and it wasn't as if they had extra bedrooms.

The look Liz received from Martha June made her shudder. MJ was furious. "And you thought Maudie should have my bedroom? Why didn't you just leave her in the closet where I told her to stay?"

"Daughter?" This was a very stern Mr. Carpenter. "You never said a word to us about this. We use that room only in an extreme emergency. It's most unpleasant. Why did you think there was one before we even left for the dance?"

MJ said nothing. She had been caught. She stared at Liz in anger and dismay.

"Martha June made a mistake," Liz said quietly, "and she tried to take care of it. But it's too serious for us to keep to ourselves, MJ. We must tell your parents."

MJ nodded slowly, defeated.

"Let's all go into my study," Mr. Carpenter said.

Mrs. Carpenter shook her head. "Tell me about it later. I must see that Maudie is all right. The poor child. She must have been terrified."

In the study, they let Martha June do most of the talking. Then Liz confessed her apprehension at leaving Maudie alone in the house, her decision to tell Nick, and their deception in leaving the dance early.

"You, at least, showed concern for another human being," Mr. Carpenter said. "Your father would be proud of you, Elizabeth. But Martha June, I am disappointed. Not only for forgetting to use discretion when it comes to mentioning our support of colored people—I can see that you didn't mean to do that, and everyone makes mistakes—but also for your lack of compassion."

"I'm sorry, Papa."

"Not knowing what has happened to Tim Webster is serious. He was so unhappy living in that household, there is no telling what he might have done with the information Martha June unwittingly gave him. I am more worried about him than his father. Mr. Webster is a hopeless drunk and probably doesn't remember what he heard—if Tim indeed told him anything.

"Thank you, Elizabeth and Nicholas, for putting Maudie ahead of yourselves. The only thing I can fault you for is not telling Mrs. Carpenter or me immediately. This is going to be very difficult for Maudie, but I'm afraid we must move quickly to transfer her to another safe house."

Liz pinched back tears. Maudie was her friend, and she might never see her again. But her safety was the important thing.

"Now, Martha June, I'd like you to join your mother. The two of you can help Maudie return to her own room, where Elizabeth will be able to comfort her later. And I expect you to give Maudie a heart-felt apology."

"Yes, Papa."

Liz was certain Maudie would forgive MJ, but would MJ forgive Liz?

As soon as Martha June had left the room, Mr. Carpenter thanked Nick again and told him he should go to bed but that Elizabeth should remain. While Nick knew of Liz's fear of being alone with the man, he couldn't very well protest, so he just nodded and said goodnight.

Then Mr. Carpenter turned to a very nervous Liz. "Elizabeth, I won't keep you for long. I can tell that you are extremely tired. But don't worry about Martha June. Before she goes to sleep, I'll let her know that both her mother and I forgive her, and I will make certain she knows not to be angry with you. Now about Maudie. You care about her, don't you?"

"Yes, she is my best friend here." Other than Nick, that was true.

"Unusual but commendable. I wish more people were as generous in spirit as you. What I'm going to tell you now is a secret. You must not tell anyone. Do you promise?"

"I promise, Mr. Carpenter." Except for Nick, of course. They couldn't have secrets.

"We believe we've located Maudie's mother. We're not certain, but we believe she has made it to Canada. And Maudie's father is traveling from station to station now and should be here soon. Thus, we can't send Maudie far from us. The Faul house is another station in the URR and has better facilities for helping her and others. We shall take Maudie there before sunrise. If we practice a great deal of care, you will see her again before she continues her journey. Would that please you?"

Liz burst out crying. The tension, the late hour, everything had finally taken its toll. "Yes, thank you, Mr. Carpenter. I think Leah is a splendid girl. She will be good to Maudie."

Mr. Carpenter smiled. "You are rather splendid yourself. Go to bed now. I'd like to talk with you about your fine father, but another time will do."

Liz nodded and made her escape, almost tripping in her eagerness to climb the stairs to her room.

Outside of Maudie's door, she could hear MJ and Mrs. Carpenter talking softly. Had MJ apologized? Would her father really forgive her? Somehow, Liz knew it would be a mistake to make an enemy of the older girl. She liked MJ well enough but sensed she should be cautious.

If only I can stay awake so I can say goodnight to Maudie, she thought. In fact, she wished she didn't have to go to sleep, period. What day would it be tomorrow? Since today was Saturday, tomorrow should be Sunday, but there were no guarantees when it came to days—at least not for her and Nicky. Would she awaken to find Maudie already gone? "If it's Sunday, I don't want to go to church. Too tired. Too tired for anything but sleep."

Chapter Nine

SHE SMELLED BACON. FOR A moment, Liz thought she was home. Sometimes Mom cooked bacon for Sunday breakfast. And waffles covered with maple syrup from Wisconsin. When had she eaten last? She couldn't recall ever being so hungry. Guess she'd better get up before Mom ate it all herself. She opened her eyes. Oh, right. Not home. Still at the Carpenters'—and no idea what day it was.

But it was too quiet. Why weren't MJ or Maudie hounding her to get dressed? It must be late, she decided. She selected a plain blue dress that might work no matter what day it turned out to be. A quick wash up, and then a peek into Maudie's room.

"Oh, no!" the room was bare of all contents, except for one lone cot and an old empty dresser. Maudie was gone, and Liz had no recollection of saying goodbye. She couldn't even ask. When she missed days, people acted as if she had been there the whole time. Instagram—snapshots, she thought, remembering Nick's theory. Each day, they caught glimpses of what life had been like back then.

But the bacon was real, and Liz rushed down to the dining table and found a different mom, Mrs. Carpenter, eating alone. "Oh, I am glad you're awake at last," Mrs. Carpenter said. "I knew you must be exhausted after yesterday and needed a good long rest. It wouldn't do for you to become ill again."

What was safe to ask? "Where's Martha June?" she asked tentatively.

Mrs. Carpenter smiled. "Such good news. She and Mr. Carpenter left for school even before sun-up. I know it was only conjecture yesterday, but it's worked out after all. The students will be able to start their school week today with a brand new teacher."

"Monday," Liz whispered.

"Monday," Mrs. Carpenter agreed. "Just as it should be, with Mr. Richards gone, thankfully, and a new teacher in place."

"Martha June is teaching?"

"Martha June is assisting," Mrs. Carpenter corrected. "That lovely Kate Dixon has agreed to teach the children. Or I should say Kate Dixon Oldfield now. I keep forgetting she married Richard Oldfield. With her husband and all four of her brothers serving in the 4th Battalion, she needs a distraction, and the teaching position will be a blessing both to her and the children. Martha June is too old to be one of the students, but perhaps old enough to assist."

"She'll learn a lot by helping," Liz said. And it might help Martha June grow up, or at least seem more her age.

"Do you want to give school another try, Lizzie?" This was the first time Mrs. Carpenter had called her that.

"I'd like to think about it," Liz answered, although it didn't appear she had many choices about what each day brought. Wait a minute, though. She and Nick had made a lot of decisions, including standing up for themselves with Mr. Richards and leaving school. They might have made a huge difference in Maudie's life, too. Maybe they did have some control over events here. Nick. Where was he? Could she ask?

"Yes, you think about it. Martha June says your school in Virginia must have been quite fine—that you knew more than others in the class. Twelve is very young not to attend school, but learning homemaking skills is important, too. Now, finish your breakfast before Mr. Carpenter and Nicholas return."

She needed to know. "Where are they?"

"Oh, I'm sorry. Of course you wouldn't know. Such a tragedy! Late last night, long after you were asleep, poor Tim's body was discovered. As you can imagine, I was frantic when Henry failed to come home. A message arrived with the news early this morning. Henry, Nicholas, and others are taking Tim back to the farm."

"How did . . ."

"How did he die? I don't know the details yet. We'll have to wait to hear. Now eat your breakfast and pack a bag for a few days. Mr. Faul will come for you soon. Leah is looking forward to having you as her guest."

So that's what was happening today. She was going to Leah Faul's farm. Did that mean she would see Maudie, too? That would be wonderful, but she hoped she would be able to talk with Nick first. It didn't seem quite safe being without him.

Nick and Mr. Carpenter returned shortly after Liz had packed a small satchel. Mr. Carpenter whispered a few words to his wife and hurried off again.

Mrs. Carpenter turned to Liz and Nick. "He's gone back to the Webster farm. I'm going out there, too, to see if I can be of comfort to Emma. This is just dreadful. Elizabeth, you have a good time at the Fauls' without worrying about any of this sorrow. I will see you in a few days. And you get some rest, Nicholas. We can't have you becoming ill on top of everything else."

"Yes, ma'am."

"You do look awful," Liz said, as soon as Mrs. Carpenter left the room.

"Well, thanks. That helps a lot."

"Sorry. Didn't mean anything."

"I know that. Sorry to be so crabby, but we were out all night. It was terrible finding him. Lizzie, he froze to death, trapped under a fallen tree branch with an empty jug beside him. I guess he decided to be like his father after all. He might have survived if he hadn't been drunk."

"Could you tell if he had been trying to . . ."

"Betray Maudie? No papers on him or anything like that. He wasn't even wearing a coat or shoes. He must have been drinking before he even left, doing something so crazy. He didn't have a chance out there in the woods." Then Nick noticed her bag. "Going somewhere?"

"Yes, I just found out. I'm going to Leah Faul's house for a few days. If Maudie is there, I guess I'll see her. But I won't see you, Nick."

"As soon as I get some sleep, I'll try to hike out there. Don't worry. Oh, wait . . ." He pulled a letter from his pocket. "It's a good thing I'm working in the post office. A letter came for you from your soldier father. Looks like you got lucky. His daughter's name is Elizabeth, too. Read it later."

"That's strange, but I guess it is a pretty common name. Did Mr. Gray send anything to Mr. Carpenter?"

"Not yet, but I'll keep looking. I don't know what I'll do if one comes, though."

Stealing mail? That was a dilemma. "Maybe there won't be anything." Quickly, Liz packed the letter out of sight. "Get some sleep now, Nick."

"Okay." He yawned. "One more thing. What day is it?"

"Monday," Liz answered, "but I don't know the date."

"Monday." Nick shrugged. "See you later, Lizzie."

Liz had never encountered a family quite like the Fauls. Large, sprawling, disorganized— but the warmest and most welcoming she had met anywhere. Their farmhouse was crammed with people, who seemed to bump into each other constantly without minding a bit. Mr. and Mrs. Faul both spoke with strong German accents, and Liz had trouble understanding them sometimes. Mr. Faul gave her an encouraging smile and Mrs. Faul such a strong embrace that Liz knew it didn't matter. Their actions communicated perfectly.

"I'm so pleased you've come," Leah said. "I've been lonely."

Liz looked around at all of the family members standing in the shabby parlor, anxiously awaiting introductions. "Lonely? Really?"

Leah laughed. "Well, lonely for someone my own age." Then she indicated, one-by-one, her sisters and a brother. "This is Catherine, Louisa, Lydia, Susan, Ella, and Lewis. Fred and Henry are serving in the Illinois Militia."

Only Ella seemed shy, hiding her face in Louisa's skirt. The others were almost boisterous in their hellos. Then the biggest surprise of all! Maudie and two other black girls burst into the room. "Lizzie!" Maudie cried. This was a Maudie Liz had never seen before. Relaxed, happy, just a girl—no longer a slave or even a servant.

"Maudie!" Liz gave her an enormous hug. The others watching might have been a little startled but not shocked as the Carpenters would have been. "Maudie, you look wonderful! Who are your friends?"

Maudie quickly introduced Bessie and Ivy. "We share a room and help with the housework and cooking," Bessie said.

"Ain't hard," Maudie added. "Ev'ryone helps here."

"With so many people underfoot, each must do his part," Lewis explained. He seemed older than the rest, although it was hard to tell.

A bell rang in the distance. "Supper," Mrs. Faul called out, and the whole crowd rushed into the enormous kitchen, where there were two tables made of long boards, with wooden benches on both sides. On the tables were platters of food. People didn't seem to have traditional seats but sat helter-skelter, including Maudie, Bessie, and Ivy. Mr. and Mrs. Faul didn't even sit at the same table. Mr. Faul gave a short grace, and then everyone began to pass the platters and chatter noisily.

Liz wondered what Maudie's cover story—her camouflage—might be here. It occurred to her that part of Maudie's protection could be that she was simply not acting like a runaway but a member of the family, although the danger of capture must always be great. While the Carpenters meant well, they had never accepted Maudie as one of them. It was like they knew slavery was wrong and that all people should be treated equally, but they hadn't quite grasped it in their hearts. If not totally safe here, Maudie was safer out of town in the country and certainly would be happier until the time her father came to continue their journey.

As far as her own security went, Liz was worried. Leah had whispered that the two of them would share a room. Liz needed to read the letter from Elizabeth's father and was hoping to talk with Nick whenever he arrived—in private. Did such a thing as privacy exist in the Faul household? At least at the Carpenters', she had her own room, far away from everyone else.

Later, in the feather bed she shared with Leah, Liz decided to be honest—or sort of honest about a few things. "Leah, before you put out the light, I need to read a letter. It's from my father, and I haven't had time to even open it."

"A letter. How exciting. Let's talk a bit, and then I'll go right to sleep. You can read your letter in private. Just be sure to blow out the candle when you're finished."

"Thanks."

Liz must have sounded relieved, for Leah gave a little laugh. "You must not have brothers and sisters. I imagine my family and its ways seem very different to you."

"Yes, but I think they're wonderful. But don't you miss having privacy?"

Leah shook her head. "You don't miss what you've never had. Normally, Susan shares this bed with me, but we've bundled her up with Ella while you're here."

"How does Susan feel about that?"

"Not pleased. Ella kicks."

Both Liz and Leah came down with a fit of the giggles, and for a few lovely moments, Liz felt like she was back home having an overnight with Danni. The thought of Danni reminded her of Maudie. "Maudie is much happier here, Leah. The Carpenters meant well, but . . ."

"She's a nice girl and has had a terrible time. She misses her mother dreadfully and hasn't seen her since she was sold and separated from Maudie. Fortunately, they both managed to escape. But don't worry about Maudie. She is never alone here, and my family won't let anything bad happen to her."

"Who are the other girls—Bessie and Ivy?"

"Freed slaves, who now work for the Underground Railroad. They've had some education and are actually older than they look. They're staying with us for a while, helping Maudie prepare for her journey ahead. They'll take her the rest of the way if her father doesn't come within the next month." Leah sighed. "But if he doesn't arrive by then, we'll have to assume something's happened to him."

Then Leah wanted to talk about the changes at school. "Once my father got Mrs. Oldfield to agree to teach, he and Mr. Carpenter fired Mr. Richards."

"Will you go back?"

"I don't know. Maybe I'll try, Lizzie, if you'll come, too. My health isn't all it should be. Sometimes I have trouble breathing."

Liz knew more than Leah about that. Leah Faul was the part she had wanted to play at the Living Cemetery, so she had studied that particular information sheet. She was disappointed when Amy got the part instead and had barely glanced at her assigned role, MJ's mother, Martha Blanchard Carpenter. Poor Leah was going to die when she was only eighteen because of breathing unhealthy air from dirt and decaying plants—the same thing that killed her little sister Martha when she was only eight months old. Liz knew it wouldn't do any good to warn Leah. There was nothing she could do about it—probably too late anyway. But it made her sad to know such a thing about a person living, lying right next to her.

"Maybe I'll give school another try," Liz said. "Anyone would be better than Mr. Richards. I don't know if I'll like having Martha June as one of my teachers, though."

"I don't know about that either," Leah said. "Hearing that she was an assistant was a surprise."

Liz gave a brief explanation of MJ's confidence. "Now I'm afraid she might be mad at me. I'm sure she didn't mean to say anything that would hurt Maudie."

"Probably not," Leah said, "but Martha June often says things she shouldn't just to get attention. You had to tell, Lizzie. What choice did you have? Think how you would have felt if Maudie had been captured."

"Awful. Thank you for understanding."

Then Liz decided to risk it. She had come up with a possible solution to one of her many problems. "Leah, I need to tell you something, but I'd like to keep it a secret so the adults won't worry." Leah nodded for her to continue. "Before I came here, I had a slight accident. At the train station in Virginia, I was sitting next to a luggage cart, and a large trunk fell on my head."

"How terrible! Were you hurt badly?"

"I think I was unconscious for a few moments. There was no one around to help me." Liz wondered if people in this time knew about concussions or used that word for them. "I did receive a . . . head injury. I'm all right, but something strange has happened since. Every morning when I wake up, I'm not certain what day it is. I'm kind of embarrassed to mention it. So tomorrow, will you tell me? I'll be confused at first, but I do better as the day goes on."

"I promise," Leah said, "and I promise not to tell anyone. Now read your letter, and I'll go to sleep. We rise early, and I'm becoming very tired."

But the letter was still in her bag on the other side of the room. Also, the room was cold, and she was toasty warm under the down comforter. Liz blew out the candle on the bedside table. The letter must wait until . . . until whatever the next day turned out to be.

Chapter Ten

"TODAY IS TUESDAY," LEAH WHISPERED to her.

"Tuesday? Wonderful!" Liz said. Unless a whole week had passed, this time she hadn't missed any days. "Yesterday was Monday, and today is Tuesday."

"Yah," Mrs. Faul said, rinsing her breakfast dishes at the sink. "Yah, Tuesday ist a fine day indeed."

Little Ella stared at Liz as if she had two heads and was a strange visitor from another planet. The only family member who seemed to find her weird was a shy four-year-old.

Catching on quickly to the routine, Liz served herself porridge from the large pot on the black stove, poured a glass of milk, and grabbed an apple from a bowl. Breakfast in the Faul household was a casual affair, which suited Liz perfectly.

Leah and the older girls were almost finished with their meal. "Papa is going to take Louisa, Lydia, Susan, and me to school. I understand that you might not want to go yet." Leah whispered that she would try to find out how Martha June felt about Liz.

Liz nodded, not sure if that was a good idea. "Be careful, though. She might have forgiven me already." And I just don't remember, she thought. That was one of the biggest problems about missing days. Things happened on those days—things she was expected to know. "My goodness, with all of you going to school, the enrollment is about to have a huge leap."

Leah grinned. "For today, anyway. We won't be able to go all the time, but Papa thinks we should show our approval and appreciation of Mrs. Oldfield, and I'm feeling well today."

Liz thought Leah's cheeks showed more color than usual.

"Oh, I forgot to tell you, Lizzie. Nick is here. He's outside talking with Lewis. I think they want you to go somewhere with them. I'm late. Papa will be angry."

It was hard to believe anyone was ever angry here, but of course that wasn't possible. Most of the time, though, Liz could tell that the people in this family tried very hard to be kind to each other and to make a happy home. Liz rinsed out her bowl, took a last swallow of milk, hoping it was safe to drink. When had pasteurization been invented? But did she really want to know? She grabbed another apple to eat on the way.

Lewis, who turned out to be fifteen, already knew Nick. They had met during the hunt for Tim Webster. Both had been given the day off work because of their efforts with the search party.

"Nick says you'd like to explore the cemetery, especially the area west of St. Joseph Creek," Lewis said. "I can show you the best place to ford it. Lucky you didn't ask last spring. The floods were so bad we couldn't even bury old Pierce there."

Liz and Nick exchanged startled glances. Old Pierce? Could Lewis possibly mean Pierce Downer, the founder of Downers Grove?

"Oh, sorry," Lewis said, misinterpreting their expressions. "Of course you don't know what I'm talking about. Old Pierce Downer died last April, but the floods almost wiped out the cemetery. My sister's grave was untouched, thank goodness, although we had to replace some of the other stones."

"We'd like it if you would show us around," Liz said. She didn't want to show too much enthusiasm. "We haven't seen much of the area."

"Sure thing," Lewis said, and they set off toward town. As much as Liz wanted to talk in private with Nick, having Lewis explain things probably would save a great deal of time. He seemed to be an interesting person, without being too interested in them. At least he didn't appear to be in the least bit nosy.

"Pierce Downer founded Downers Grove back in 1832. He came here from the East, made friends with the Pottawatomie Indians, and decided to stay."

"Grove," Liz said, looking around. "Because of all the maple trees, right?"

"Oak trees," Lewis said. "There are actually more oaks than maples in Downers Grove, although the maples are out-performing the oaks at the moment."

"They're gorgeous," Liz said. "But so are the oaks. That's one reason I want to return to the cemetery. I fell in love with an amazing oak tree there."

"I know exactly the one you mean. It's been there even longer than the first settlers. Mr. Carpenter is really the one responsible for the cemetery. He talked Sam Curtiss into selling part of his cow pasture. Eventually the town will pay $15.00 for the land—too much, of course, but perhaps worth it. Mr. Carpenter will be president of the Burying Ground Association."

"Mr. Carpenter seems to be in charge of a lot of what goes on here," Nick said.

"Yes, he and Pops take on a great deal."

"I like the way almost everyone in town pitches in to make it work," Liz said. It seemed to be more of a democracy here than what she had been used to. Every member of Lewis's family, plus the other families of the community, put forth effort to make the town and their homes function. If Dad were gone for good, she and Mom needed to be better at making their home happier—not like the Fauls', but their own kind of happy. At least she was willing to try now, if only she had the opportunity.

"There's the blacksmith shop," Lewis pointed out. "And there's Mr. Thatcher's and Mr. Hatch's, although most of us prefer Mr. Carpenter's general store. We could surely use an apothecary, though."

"Walgreens," Nick whispered, seeing Liz's puzzled look.

Finally, they reached the cemetery. Not the cleared, carefully protected place Liz and Nick knew, although their last trip had prepared them. First, they visited the gravestone of little Martha Faul. Lewis bowed his head and looked solemn. "She was the sweetest baby you ever saw," he said. "None of us ever got over her death. That's probably one of the reasons we spoil Ella. Although she's so good, she won't let us completely spoil her."

"You can't spoil someone by loving them," Nick said.

Did she know Nick at all? The Nick in 2011, that is. All she had known in their time was that he was cute, popular, and she wanted him to be her date for the dance. Did he have two parents and brothers and sisters? She had never thought about it before. He didn't know anything about her, either. She wondered if he even cared.

"Martha was the first person buried here," Lewis continued. "I suppose it is an honor."

"I'm certain it is," Liz said. "I'll bet the people of this town will remember her for hundreds of years. And the other people buried here as well."

Lewis smiled and said that while he doubted that, it did sound grand. Then he showed her other gravesites. "I knew some of these people. No doubt I'll know even more soon, thanks to this war. Of course, I'm almost sixteen and will enlist. Someday, perhaps, mine will be one of the graves people visit."

Time to change the subject, Liz decided. Too depressing. "Oh, there's my tree!" She ran to it. Its thick, dark brown bark seemed to offer protection from all the death surrounding her. She wished she could climb to the top and survey the whole area. She might have been tempted had she been alone, but she wouldn't feel comfortable wearing a dress with the boys watching from below. Instead, she looked up at the dozens of branches wearing their autumn colors of yellow, bronze, and red. Soon the leaves would rain down and cover many of the graves, keeping them safe from the cold until snow provided a different blanket. Would she still be here to see it then? Did she want to be? Lovingly, she patted the tree, but that broke the spell. She withdrew her hand quickly and stared at the sticky goo covering it.

Lewis laughed while handing her a rag from his pocket. "I never go anywhere without one."

"It's getting late," Nick said. "We'd better take a look at the creek."

Liz was familiar with St. Joseph Creek. She knew it was located west of town, in Woodridge and Lisle, but it must be on the east side, too. It had caused some flooding problems to homes near Hummer Park on Fairview Avenue. But it certainly wasn't anywhere near the cemetery during her time, unless it flowed underground. As it turned out, the creek had a mind of its own even back then.

"The stream decided to change directions last spring." Lewis chuckled. "That's why we have to enter through the back now."

"But . . ." Liz caught herself from saying, "But it is the front. That's the way we always come in. The entrance is on Main Street." For the first time, though, she noticed that the gravestones all faced west—not east, where Main Street was located in her time. Now, Union Street was west of the creek, past where she thought she had last seen the pavilion. She wondered if more flooding had eventually meant changing the location of the main street of the town.

"Now to ford the creek," Lewis said. "Using Lizzie's tree as a marker, go straight west, and there you'll find the safest place to cross."

Because of a few decent steppingstones and it being the narrowest part of the creek, Liz felt confident crossing over, even wearing a cumbersome skirt. Three steps were all it took for Nick and Lewis to reach the other side. Lewis held out his hand, which she accepted—the last stone did look slippery. Such a disappointment once there—brush and more trees. How would they ever find the pavilion?

Nick spoke to both of them but looked at Liz. "I'd like to come back and explore another time, but I think we'd better leave. School should be out soon, and it's getting dark early. It's a long walk to the farm. You'll want to catch a ride from Mr. Faul."

Lewis agreed. "And I must help Pops with the evening chores," he said.

At least they had learned where and how to cross the creek. Somehow, she and Nick had to figure out where a pavilion would be located almost one hundred and fifty years later.

On the way to the schoolhouse, Nick said that Mr. Carpenter had invited him to attend a meeting of abolitionists—for those working on the Underground Railroad.

"I'd like to go, too."

Lewis shook his head. "Sorry, Lizzie, but no women are allowed at URR meetings." Liz bristled. "No it isn't fair, but Nick and I will fill you in."

"And perhaps you'll be able to spend some time with Maudie tonight," Nick said, trying to make her feel better.

Liz nodded. She didn't like it but knew there wasn't anything she could do. At least, she didn't think there was.

Back at the farm, Leah couldn't rave enough about her school day. "You missed all the fun, Lizzie. Mrs. Oldfield is lovely, and Martha June acted all grown up. You wouldn't have known she was the same person."

"Was she nice to everyone?"

"Oh, yes, and helpful, too. The boys who used to be dreadful to Mr. Richards were well behaved. I didn't know they knew how to be good. Mrs. Oldfield doesn't even have a whip or cane in the classroom. She said she doesn't believe in hitting children."

"Zat vill not last long." Mrs. Faul hustled them into the kitchen. "Zey vill return to old ways soon. You kinder talk later. Now help fix supper. Lizzie and Lewis must eat much after missing dinner."

"Where's Maudie?" Lizzie wondered, not just because she wanted to know, but also to change the subject. She didn't want questions about why she and Lewis had been absent for the noon meal. Leah, of course, had eaten at school.

"Mit Bessie and Ivy," Mrs. Faul answered. "I do not know vere."

Liz hoped Maudie hadn't left without saying goodbye, but it would be useless to question Mrs. Faul further. Instead, she proceeded to help Leah and her sisters. If everyone was to eat, there was work to be done. Liz offered to peel the potatoes. She was good at making potato salad. Cold meat and fresh fruit would also be served. Mrs. Faul had baked bread from cornmeal that had come from nearby Graue Mill. "Tomorrow, you vill bake zee bread, Lizzie," she said. Fortunately, tomorrow was another day—that is, sometimes, Liz thought.

It wasn't until after supper when Leah offered to read to her younger sisters that Liz finally had time to go to the shared bedroom and read the letter from Elizabeth Gray's father.

My dear daughter,

I pray that you are well and happy in your new situation. I did receive a wire from Henry Carpenter advising me that you had arrived safely. I will be forever grateful to him and his family.

I am doing the work God meant me to do—helping to keep our beloved country united, and making certain that all of our citizens, no matter their color, are free and are treated fairly. It grieves me that our home state takes an opposing view.

Even though I'm doing what I must, realize that I regret every moment we're apart. I am proud of you— especially right now— for your courage at facing far more than any young girl should have to alone. I know that if your darling mother were here, she would be proud, too. She in heaven and me here in no man's land—both of us applaud you.

Take very good care of yourself, and do help the Carpenters as much as you're able. May we be together again soon.

Your loving father,
Charles W. Gray, Major, Union forces, U.S. Army

Liz started to cry—she wasn't sure why. From guilt, perhaps. Most definitely from longing. She envied the real Elizabeth Gray, wherever she was. Why couldn't Liz Havelka's dad be like that? He didn't even care enough to send support money to her mother or a birthday card to her. Then Liz stopped crying as something frightening occured to her. Elizabeth Gray. Was she okay or in terrible danger? She belonged here, not Liz Havelka. Would her loving father ever see his daughter, the real Elizabeth Gray, again?

"Lizzie? Are you all right? You've been crying."

"I'm fine. It's just . . . well, I miss my father. He wrote me such a wonderful letter, and I'm hoping he'll be safe."

Leah gave her a hug. "Yes, that's what I'm hoping about my brothers— what we're all hoping about so many men. That they'll be safe and home soon. The war seems so far away from here, but I don't suppose it is, really."

Once in bed that night, Leah talked more about school. "I won't be able to go tomorrow because Papa needs the horse and cart, and he doesn't want me to overdo. Sometimes I think I breathe easier when I'm in town, though."

Because the air is cleaner, Liz thought, although she didn't say anything. It wasn't like Leah could move away. "I'll give school another try," she promised. "Tell me more about Martha June. Did she say anything about me?"

"Yes, and don't worry, Lizzie, I was tactful. She said you didn't have a choice when you saw that Maudie was in danger. She doesn't blame you, and her father has forgiven her."

"I am relieved," Liz said.

"It's probably best that you don't mention Maudie to Martha June, though. Mr. Carpenter told her that Maudie's father came and that they are on their way north. No one else but you and Nick know that Maudie is here."

"I won't tell anyone," Liz said.

After reminding Leah to be sure to let her know what day it was the next morning, she blew out the candle.

But Liz couldn't sleep. She was restless, unhappy, not certain what to do next. Hardest of all, she no longer knew what she wanted. In so many ways, her life here was more meaningful. Back home in her own time, it was all about hanging out with friends and owning things and figuring out how— not to disobey rules exactly, but definitely how to get around them. All she and her friends wanted was to have fun. Good times were important here, too, but ideas of what was fun were simpler, and more was at stake. It was about everyone doing their part. It was about helping each other. It was about survival. If she were to return, would she go back to her old ways, or would some of Elizabeth Gray return with her? And Nicky . . . Would she go back to thinking of him as just another cute boy she needed to trick into asking her to a dance? Or would he continue to be the best friend he had become? And most important and troubling were Mom and Dad. What kind of future could she have with them?

Chapter Eleven

MAUDIE HAD RETURNED WITH BESSIE and Ivy the next day, which was, Liz discovered to her great relief, Wednesday. Perhaps time had finally settled down, and the days would now progress in an orderly fashion. She learned that because there had been reports of slave hunters in the area, the three girls had spent the previous day in hiding. All seemed to be well now—for the moment. Liz also learned that the Carpenters had requested that she remain with the Fauls until the weekend. Mr. Carpenter was out of town, Mrs. Carpenter wasn't feeling well, and Martha June had her new teaching duties. This suited Liz just fine. If it weren't for Nick, she would prefer staying with Leah and her family until she could go home. But other than Nick, there was also the cemetery. It was quite a distance from the Fauls' farm but a relatively easy hike from the Carpenters' house on Maple Avenue.

Bubbling over with excitement, Maudie had received word that her father would arrive soon and that both of them would continue as passengers on their way to freedom. "I would like to meet your father, Maudie," Liz said. From the look on Maudie's face, Liz knew she couldn't have said anything that would please her friend more.

"You will like Poppy." Then, after a long pause, "Ah will miss you, Lizzie."

"I'll miss you even more. But if you're finally safe and free, it will be worth it."

No, she would never see Maudie again. Once she and Nick returned to their own time, though, she wouldn't see her anyway—or Leah and her sisters and Lewis—or Martha June. Now that Martha June was a teacher, would she still want to be called MJ?

Today was chore day, Mrs. Faul announced, smiling when her children loudly groaned and proclaimed that every day was chore day. The older ones had already been hard at work since dawn—feeding livestock, gathering eggs, and raking leaves for mulch. Soon Liz was to discover just how difficult it was to live on a working farm as she began the longest and most educational day of her life. First, she contributed to dinner by making cornbread—and not from a mix purchased at a local supermarket. She learned that Graue Mill, where the cornmeal was ground, was named for Mr. Faul's relative, Frederick Graue, also a German immigrant. In 1852, he and his partner had built the gristmill in Brush Hill. How she wished she could tell them that the mill still had their relative's name and that it still functioned in 2011.

Fortunately, by following Leah's careful directions, making cornbread from scratch wasn't difficult. Using unbleached flour, cornmeal, salt saleratus (baking soda), molasses, eggs, and buttermilk, Liz's cornbread was soon rising in the cavernous black oven.

During this time, Maudie was ironing, using two black irons so heavy Liz had trouble lifting them. She saw quickly why there were two. While Maudie ironed with one, the other was heating on the stove. Both irons had wooden handles, keeping Maudie from being burned. If they were made of the same material as the irons, the heat would have scalded her poor hands. But were irons made of iron? Is that why irons and ironing were called that? Back home, Liz and her mother seldom used the electric iron. Mom's new clothes dryer tossed the damp clothes until they were wrinkle free.

After the cornbread was done, Liz found, to her amazement, she was expected to help make homemade butter out in the shed attached to the farmhouse. She watched Mr. Faul turn the handle on a wooden barrel contraption like ones she'd seen at Graue Mill but had never thought much about. Almost effortlessly, he continued to churn the heavy cream. Then he told her to give it a try. Liz tried. In fact, she turned until she thought her arm would fall off. It was exhausting.

"Here it comes now," Mr. Faul said, unscrewing the top of the butter churn. "Now you women must take over." He left the shed to tackle other chores.

"Look, Lizzie, the butter has gathered." Catherine, the eldest sister, pulled the plug from the bottom of the churn while Liz watched the buttermilk spout into a pail. Soon, using wooden paddles, Catherine added salt before forming mounds of golden butter. "Now, use your hands. Just pretend you're working with clay, and make pats of butter."

At first it seemed as if her hands didn't belong to her, but she soon got the hang of it. Liz thought she had never been so proud of anything. It was like magic and once spread on the cornbread would be absolutely delicious.

That was Liz's contribution to dinner. Ham and brown beans made up the rest of the meal, but Liz was convinced the tastiest part was her cornbread and butter. Mr. Faul had brought home a can of tinned milk for them to try. This was a new item in Mr. Hatcher's store, and they all drank just a little. Liz wondered which was safer—milk from a cow or from a can? Probably neither was a good idea. Louisa had made a pie and a lemon cake, but it was agreed that her treats would taste much better at suppertime. Everyone was too full for anything heavy and settled for Mrs. Faul's home-canned cherries.

Liz was exhausted by the time they brought water from the well, heated it on the stove, and washed the dishes. Perhaps they would rest after dinner? No, not on a farm. Louisa insisted that her sisters help her weave. Lizzie had never done that, but she could watch and perhaps help next time.

There were clothes for sale in Mr. Carpenter's store—mainly outdoor coats and boots for men and boys. While Liz preferred her clothes in 2011, both for style and comfort and would rather buy them at the mall, she did appreciate MJ's cast-offs. She had never thought about where clothing actually came from. In an attic room of the farm, she was introduced to the weaving loom and spinning wheel. She had seen both, of course, at Graue Mill and at Naper Settlement, but her friends here used them out of necessity.

Louisa was working the loom that day, weaving material for winter coats for the older family members who had outgrown theirs. Little Ella rarely had new clothing, but Leah was making her a rag doll as a birthday surprise. With the child napping, she was able to work on it away from prying eyes. Liz knew that Ella owned the beautiful porcelain doll that had been her mother's. It sat in its own rocking chair—far too valuable and breakable for a plaything.

Liz preferred watching Louisa to helping Maudie and Mrs. Faul use a washboard to scrub clothes in a large tub. At least she knew what a washboard was. Mrs. Lester had one in the props cabinet at school.

By the time Nick came to see her late afternoon, on the pretense of visiting Lewis, Liz felt as if a whole week had passed. Nick, too, had had a busy day. "I finally saw some money," he said. "They're called greenbacks and look like a bigger version of our dollar bill. People don't seem to trust greenbacks much. Mr. Carpenter operates mainly by credit. I don't know how he gets paid. He took me to the blacksmith shop. That was amazing. I thought blacksmiths only put new shoes on horses, but they do other things, too, like make iron pots and repair plows and tools. Mr. Carpenter needed some of his tools mended. I didn't have time to go back to the cemetery, though."

"Maybe tomorrow," Liz said. "Did any mail come for Mr. Carpenter?"

"You mean from your father? No, not yet."

"I wonder what happened to Elizabeth—if she's all right."

Nick stared at her. "I never thought of that. I guess I hope so, too, as long as she doesn't get here before we leave. The month must be almost over. I'm not sure they celebrate Halloween. If they do, it won't be the same way we're used to."

"I haven't seen the date since Mr. Richards wrote in on the blackboard, and I have a hard enough time keeping track of the days of the week. But Nick, I have this feeling that we must return by Halloween. I don't know why. I'm just afraid that if we don't, we never will."

"No matter what, Lizzie, we'll go to the cemetery tomorrow."

Lewis interrupted, insisting that Nick come out to the barn to see the new colt. "And Lizzie, Leah is looking for you. Something about trying a new hairstyle she learned about in school."

"Thanks. I'll go now."

Leah, Susan, Maudie, and Ella had gathered in Leah's bedroom. "It's called a chignon, Lizzie," Leah said. "All the girls at school are wearing theirs this way. Can you guess what language chignon is?"

"French, isn't it?" Liz said, although she knew very well it was and had worn her hair in a chignon many times—before she had chopped it off and dyed it pink. She refrained from grinning but thought Leah and Susan looked as if they'd suddenly turned into little old ladies.

"You are so smart," Leah said. "Well, sit down. First, we have to brush out those messy curls and wrap your hair into a knot at the back of your head. It's very stylish and will show proper respect for Union soldiers."

Liz didn't know how a hairstyle could do that but didn't argue. Besides, she was tired of dealing with sausage curls. The chignons she had worn were much fancier than what Leah and Susan had created, but no matter. "Sometimes I think I'd rather be bald," she said, after Leah had added years to her age with the ugly bun. Maudie giggling, though, gave her an idea.

"Maudie, I am going to fix your hair the way my friend Danni wears hers. You'll be our very own Belle of the Barnyard."

"Oh, no, Lizzie, I dasn't."

"You won't do anything. I will. Just sit right there and be very, very patient. Now, Leah, I need ribbons, if you have them, preferably different colors. Beads would be great, too."

"I have ribbons," Ella said. "I'll get them. I want Maudie to be the Belle of the Barnyard."

"Wow! Way to go, Ella!" Liz cried, forgetting what year it was. "I didn't know Ella could say one whole sentence, never mind three."

Maudie sat at the dressing table facing a small mirror. "Now, Maudie, this is going to take a long time, and Leah, as soon as you figure out what I'm doing, you can start working on Maudie's other side. Back home, my friend Danni goes to a hairdresser to have her hair braided in cornrows. It costs a lot of money, but it lasts for several weeks." Liz laughed. "Danni doesn't undo it until her scalp starts itching, and she is desperate for a shampoo." She stopped when she saw everyone staring at her. How many mistakes had she just made?

Leah burst out laughing. "You are a such joker, Lizzie. A colored girl in Virginia spending money for a fancy hairstyle? Being a slave in Virginia must be a very fine thing indeed. Why, I wonder, would anyone want to be free?"

Liz gave a sheepish smile. "I guess I do let my imagination run away with me sometimes," she admitted.

"What's shampoo?" Ella asked, her hands full of colorful ribbons.

"Oh, I know that," Susan said. "I heard about it from Emma, who went to New York City last summer. It's a fancy liquid soap, just for washing your hair. We're certain to have it here someday."

Soap just for washing hair! The girls looked at each other in amazement. The world was full of wonders.

"You'll be my assistant," Liz told a delighted Ella. "Each time I finish making a tiny braid in Maudie's hair, hand me a ribbon. I could make them more secure with beads and rubber bands . . . Oh, never mind," she answered their questioning looks. "Let's get started. Maybe you could teach me some songs while we're working."

While Liz and Leah, once she got the hang of it, turned Maudie's hair into a great number of tiny braids, the girls sang the popular songs of the day, mainly war songs. "The Bonnie Blue Flag" and the "Battle Cry of Freedom" were new to Lizzie. She joined in on "The Battle Hymn of the Republic," at least on the *Glory, Glory, Hallelujah* part and also "Sweet and Low," which she had sung in the school choir. Maudie taught them "We are Coming Father Abr'am" and "Let My People Go." Then all but Liz, who didn't know the hymn, sang "Abide with Me."

> *Abide with me, fast falls the eventide*
> *The darkness deepens; Lord, with me abide*
> *When other helpers fail and comforts flee*
> *Help of the helpless, oh, abide with me.*

They sang other verses as well, sweetly, beautifully, even Ella sang. When they finished, Liz was sniffling.

"You're crying, Lizzie, why?" Susan asked.

"I'm not sure," Liz said. "You just sounded so beautiful." But Liz knew why. She was crying for all of them—because of the dangers and sorrows that lay ahead. For Maudie and her father on their perilous journey to freedom. For Leah, who would die in a few years with her family left behind to grieve. Most of all for Nick and herself, so far away from their true lives. She accepted Leah's handkerchief, giving one last sniffle.

"There," she announced grandly. "What do you think of your friend Maudie now? Doesn't she look like an African princess? All she needs is an exotic dress, preferably orange, rust, and brown, and on her head, a turban encircled with exotic fruits." Okay, so she was thinking of Danni's family's

Kwanzaa celebrations. "I'm very sorry, Princess Maudie, but we don't seem to have such attire in the castle today."

They all hooted with laughter. "Oh, Lizzie," Leah said. "Life wasn't nearly so much fun before you came. I wish you didn't have to go back to the Carpenters'."

"We'll still see each other. I'd like to stay, but I should see for myself that Martha June and I are back on good terms." Not to mention being closer to Nick and the cemetery, she added silently. But she certainly felt more at home with the Fauls, in spite of this family being so different from her own. Maybe too comfortable, if she was going to continue saying ridiculous things.

"I like Maudie being a princess, Lizzie," Susan said, "but will she leave her hair like that until her scalp itches?"

"Not unless she wants to look like a wild, untrimmed shrub. It's going to look a bit bushy anyway when we take out the braids. Let's leave them until your mother has a chance to see."

Maudie agreed. "And Bessie and Ivy," she said.

"Me, next," Ella insisted. "I want to be a princess, too."

Liz considered the little girl's hair. "Well, Maudie's style won't work for you. Your hair is too fine to hold all those little braids. I know. You can be a French princess instead of an African one. Maudie is a visiting princess from another land, and the rest of us in our plain French chignons are peasants, servants to Princess Mademoiselle Ella. We aim to serve you, Princess." Liz bowed deeply and insisted that her sisters bow, too. "Not Princess Maudie, though. Princess Maudie must never bow to anyone. Not ever again. Do you understand?"

Maudie nodded gravely. She understood.

Soon, thanks to all of the times Liz had practiced back home, little Ella was sporting a new look in French braids. Liz giggled inwardly. They must think that Virginia was more fashionable than Paris—or even New York City!

Nick had been invited for supper. He dutifully admired all of the hairdos, even the chignons, which he pronounced practical if not glamorous. He bowed down to the Princess of France, and then, frankly, stared at Maudie and then at Liz, who nodded. "Danni," she mouthed. Maudie looked almost exactly like Dannisha.

Only the older sisters, Catherine and Louisa, seemed doubtful of Maudie's hairdo. "As long as you aren't going anywhere," Catherine said. "But once you leave, you must not attract attention."

"Maudie just wants Bessie and Ivy to see her first," Liz said, "and then I'll take out the braids."

Leah's mother gave Maudie a hug. "You vas never meant to appear plain."

And when Bessie and Ivy arrived late evening, they, too, were amazed. "Maudie, you be a beauty," Ivy said. Both women raved, causing her to look away in pleased embarrassment.

Bessie sighed jealously. "Lizzie must make us beautiful, too." Liz, who knew that Maudie's cocoa-colored skin and high, prominent cheek bones did more for her looks than a complicated hairstyle ever could, promised that she would try someday soon. Would the women still be here when she visited again? Their presence was erratic. Leah had told her that they were important workers in the Underground Railroad, although she wasn't certain exactly what they did.

By the time Liz blew out the candle that night, she had decided that going back to the Carpenters' might be okay. The Faul family was terrific, but to have to work this hard every day might be too much. Although much less interesting, life certainly was easier in town.

Chapter Twelve

WHETHER OR NOT THE THOUGHT before she went to bed influenced the next day, Liz had no way of knowing. By rights, it should be Thursday. Instead, to her dismay, it was Saturday, the day she would return to town. But with any luck, perhaps she and Nick could pay another trip to the cemetery. After breakfast, Mr. Faul hitched up the buckboard wagon and after many hugs, thank yous, and a few tears from Ella, Liz got on board. She waved back at them until they rounded the bend. She had promised to return and truly hoped she could keep that promise.

"I wonder when Maudie's father will come," she said, not certain of an answer from the driver, Mr. Faul.

"Yah. Das ist somesing to vonder. Ve grow vorried for him." Liz thought there might be more at stake than just concern about Maudie. Her puzzlement must have shown for he explained, "Maudie's fader ist conductor. Many lives at risk."

Conductor of the Underground Railroad was what Mr. Faul meant. Maudie's father—she wished she knew his name—was helping slaves escape from the South. This made everything even more dangerous than she had imagined.

They were silent much of the way back. Although a kind man, Mr. Faul didn't have much use for idle conversation. He had already said a great deal—

for him. Then, "Here, Miss Lizzie, I vant a smoke." And to Liz's horror, he handed her the reins.

"Me?" she gasped.

"Not drive before?" She shook her head. "Vell, jest don't tell Old Gordon here. But he ist a fine boy and won't much care who ist his conductor. He could make trip to town and back if he vere to go blind."

There was nothing to do but hold the reins, try to act confident, and let Old Gordon proceed. When they pulled up in front of the Carpenter house and Liz returned the reins to Mr. Faul, she had to admit that other than baking cornbread and churning butter, she had never been prouder of anything. Even more special than her great part in last year's play, she had driven the Fauls' answer to a minivan!

Mr. Faul carried her bag up to the front porch. "Ve miss you. Come gud back."

"Thank you, Mr. Faul. I loved being on the farm. But my father wanted me to stay here. I don't want to go against his wishes or hurt the Carpenters' feelings."

"You gud girl. I understand, and Lizzie, you make zee best cornbread."

Liz gave him a slight wave and opened the door into—nothing. At least, no people were about. Finally, she found Mrs. Carpenter in her sewing room, sitting back in a chair with a wet cloth on her forehead.

"Oh, hello, dear. You've returned."

"Is something wrong, Mrs. Carpenter?"

"A headache. I get them fairly often."

Liz almost said, "My mother does, too," but stopped herself in time. Instead—"Is there anything I can do to help?"

"No, you run along. I'll be fine in a few hours."

"Where is Martha June?"

"Visiting, I believe. Please close the door when you leave."

Liz felt empty. She had gone from too many people to too few—from too much work to not any. On balance now, she thought she might prefer too much. At least at the farm, work included laughter, fun, and excitement. Everything there seemed important and meaningful. Perhaps she would go back to the Fauls'. But the nearby cemetery was a key to returning home, as much as the real key she still wore around her neck.

After hanging her clothes in the closet, checking that the costumes were still concealed in a corner, she went searching for Nick and was rewarded to find him in the store.

"Lizzie, you're back."

"Yes, although you may be the only reason I'm glad about that."

He smiled. "A bit different here, huh?"

"A lot different. There's nothing for me to do. Mrs. Carpenter has a headache and wants to be alone, and Martha June is visiting. And it's Saturday. I've lost track of two whole days. What about you?"

"I missed Thursday," Nick said, "but I managed to squeeze in yesterday. There's no use worrying about it, Liz. It's out of our control. Just take it as it comes. Look, I'm supposed to work here in the store and post office for a few more hours. Someone else will take over this afternoon. Why don't you hang around? We'll grab something to eat for a picnic at the cemetery. It looks as if it might rain later, but we should make it there and back before it does."

Nick had very few customers for a Saturday morning. He told Liz that many people shopped at the Thatcher and Hatch store in town. "Supposed to have a better selection of things. More modern, people say. Like the new canned milk."

Liz made a face. "I tried it. Yuck!"

She spent the time exploring both the shop and the post office. No mail had come for Mr. Carpenter, and there was no mail delivery on Saturday. She examined some of the postage stamps, which bore little resemblance to what she was used to. It cost five cents to mail a letter, which was more than what she would have expected. Maybe it cost more because of needing to rely on the pony express. And, of course, she didn't know what five cents was worth in 1863. Then she looked at the greenbacks some of the residents distrusted. They didn't seem that different from the money she was used to. Seeing Abraham Lincoln's face printed on a ten-dollar note was comforting—made her feel more at home. The money she liked best were the coins, especially the anti-slavery halfpenny tokens. The purpose of the tokens was to call attention to the plight of slaves and could be used in some places instead of the official currency. The 1863 coin was cool, but Liz was drawn to an earlier 1838 one, picturing a kneeling woman bound in chains with the legend, "Am I Not a Woman and a Sister?"

"You are my sister, Maudie," Liz whispered, shuddering at the thought of Maudie in chains.

Nick interrupted her thoughts. "Oh, Lizzie, maybe you haven't heard, but later this evening is Tim Webster's funeral service at the Congregational Church, where his mother is a member. I don't know if we're supposed to go, but we'd better make sure we're back here for supper, just in case."

"Poor Tim. Do they know yet what really happened?"

Nick shook his head. "And no one knows if Tim ever told his father what Martha June told him. I'm sure Maudie was in danger that night, but the mystery is if the Websters had anything to do with it."

Liz decided to make herself useful by figuring out what in the store they could take for lunch. It wasn't as if she could whip up a sandwich. She had a brief longing for McDonald's, or at least somewhere you could just order what you wanted, and it would magically appear. Oh, for a Big Mac, large fries, and a chocolate shake right this minute. Or dinner with the Fauls would be nice, too. The noon meal didn't seem as important to the Carpenters. All would fend for themselves.

So what could they eat? Molasses? Not likely. A barrel of flour? All the herbs and spices wouldn't do them much good. Candy might be welcome later. Had she enjoyed any of Louisa's pie and cake? Hard to say what she'd eaten on Thursday and Friday. This week, those days hadn't existed in her strange world.

Finally, Liz settled on hunks of cheese, some husk-type of bread, and fruit to keep them from being thirsty. She zipped into the kitchen for two apples, and then wrapped everything in a kind of waxed paper before putting the package into a string bag.

When Nick finally said they could go, she held out the bag and announced, "Luncheon is served, Sir Nicholas."

"Looks good. Now let's get out of here."

"Can we leave without waiting for your replacement?"

"That's what I was told. Mr. Carpenter said not to worry about it. He wasn't expecting much business this afternoon anyway, and if anyone were to come by, they'd just write what they took in the book."

"Seems awfully careless."

"I think most of his money must come from his shoe making and repair business in town. But I had an odd thought, Lizzie. I'll need to think more about it. Mr. Carpenter didn't just suggest I not be here, he insisted I be gone by noon. This has happened before. He also said he was expecting a freight delivery but that someone else would handle it. I'm thinking the store could be a front for something."

Liz gasped. "Like drugs or weapons?" That's what it usually meant back home if someone said a store was a front.

"Not exactly. But I don't think the real business of this store is selling things."

She shrugged. It couldn't be that important. The Carpenters were hardly the criminal type. "Well, we have our own business to take care of right now. We have a creek to ford. Maybe this time we'll find something."

"Do you have the key, Lizzie?"

"Always," she said.

Chapter Thirteen

"DARNED ALL THIS MATERIAL! SHOOT! Crap!" Liz cried, as she became the victim of an unprovoked attack by a sticker bush.

Nick looked around cautiously before grinning. "Careful, kid. You're forgetting who and where you are."

"Not to mention when I are. Nick, you are so lucky not having to wear these awful skirts and petticoats."

Looking down at his simple pants and jacket, Nick just missed stepping into a pile of manure. "You're right about that, although I'm not a big fan of suspenders. At least they prevent a display of my weird underwear. Lizzie, what do you miss most about back home?"

"Fast food and jeans," was her instant reply. "Oh, and Danni and my other friends talking on the phone, taking each other's pictures, overnights, going to the movies, rehearsals . . ."

"Your family?"

"Mom and I weren't getting along very well, but yeah, I miss her. Most of all, I'm worried about her missing me. She must be scared stiff."

"Is your mom your whole family?"

"Since Dad moved out for the millionth time. I wish they'd get a divorce and have it over with. I get sick of all the arguments and threats, and then he leaves and comes back, and it all starts again. It's boring." And frightening, Liz admitted to herself.

"I'm sorry. I didn't know."

"No, I keep it kinda quiet. What about you, Nicky? What do you miss most?"

"Well, I do miss my family. We're a large noisy crew—not as large as Leah's family but big enough. Other than Mom and Dad, I have two younger brothers and a little sister. My brothers are identical twins, who fight with each other constantly, but if anyone outside messes with one, he'll have the other to deal with. They're ten. And my little sister, Karen, is three. She's the only girl, so we spoil her some. And I miss my dog Alfie. He's just a mongrel from the shelter, but we've had him for eight years, and he loves me more than anyone. I'll bet he senses that I'll return someday."

"That's nice. I don't have any pets. Mom's allergic." Talking with Nick was making the walk to the cemetery go faster. His family was completely different from hers, but at least she knew more about him now. He grabbed her arm as she started to trip over a small rock. "Thanks. Something to add to the list. I miss sidewalks."

"And the absence of horse manure. But what will you miss when we do go back? What will you miss about being here? At this time, I mean."

Liz thought for a moment. "I'll miss Maudie, Leah, and the rest of the Faul family most. I got kind of exhausted being a part of them, but it was pretty wonderful, too. I've never felt so used, but I mean in a good way. I would have stayed there, but it was too far away from you and the cemetery."

"A whole hour's walk, if the weather is decent. What about Martha June? Will you miss her?"

"I don't know yet. I was starting to like her, and then that night happened. We haven't had any time together since. Leah told me MJ isn't mad at me, but I need to hear her say it. More than anything, Nick, I'll miss being involved in something so important—the war and ending slavery. It's so close to us—not the way it is in the South, of course, but still . . ."

Nick nodded. "There are wars at home, but they are so far away that most of the time we don't even think about them. Some weeks there aren't even any articles in the Trib. Iraq? Afghanistan? Most kids can't even find those places on a map. Unless you know someone in the services, war doesn't seem to touch us. I'll miss working in the store and post office and being given adult responsibilities. Being in the search party for Tim was an incredible experience, even though it was frightening. I like Mr. Carpenter and Lewis and the rest of the Faul family, but I haven't made friends the way you have. As far as people go, I guess I'll miss you the most."

"Me? But I'll be there."

"Will you? Will Lizzie Gray and Liz Havelka be the same person?"

It was a good question and couldn't really be answered. And what about Nicky and Nicholas? Were they two different people or just one? "I think I'll become a blend of both girls," she said. "I'm sure some of Elizabeth Gray will return with me."

"Then let's make sure we make it. Look, Lizzie, we're here."

More leaves covered the ground since the last time they had visited. Many of the trees displayed bare branches now, but not her mighty oak, still shining with bright leaves, the largest and most majestic presence in the whole cemetery. This time there were other people on the site, checking the various plots, clearing leaves from plaques and, in general, tidying up. This time, too, Liz and Nick recognized more of the surnames. They bowed their heads over little Martha Faul's stone. In only five years, Leah would be buried near her. They stopped also at the resting places of Walter and William H. Carpenter. How different Martha June and her family would be if her two brothers had lived.

"I'll be buried close by soon," Nick said.

"What?"

"Sorry, I didn't mean me. I meant the man I was supposed to be for the Living Cemetery—Mrs. Carpenter's brother, Walter Blanchard. He's going to be killed in late November in 1863. They'll never know the exact date. It happened at the Battle of Chattanooga."

"Poor Mrs. Carpenter. I don't want to be here when that happens, Nick."

"Me, neither."

They sat under Liz's oak tree to eat their lunch. "I don't think it's alive in our time."

"It isn't. None of the trees in our cemetery are this old, and there aren't any as tall."

"I love it. Let's make it our special, emergency meeting place. If anything goes wrong and we have to get out fast, we'll meet right here."

"Okay. And then we'll ford the stream together. I've been trying to remember that morning, Lizzie. When we reached the pavilion, it was exactly 8:45 in the morning. I looked at my watch. Hope it's back home with my clothes; my grandfather gave it me. Also I remember where the sun was then. We can cross the creek today, but I think we should come back early some morning and look again. We might have better luck."

"And we should bring the costumes with us."

"Ow!" a loud voice interrupted them.

"Who's there?" Liz demanded.

Martha June, favoring her ankle, appeared from behind the tree. "Lizzie? I didn't expect to see you here. Hello, Nick."

"Martha June? Where did you come from?" How much had she heard?

"From over there," and she pointed to an area not far away. "I thought I heard voices, and I came to check. Then I tripped over a root."

"Oh. Nick and I just decided to take a walk. There was no one home but your mother, and she has a headache, so I packed a little picnic. Is your ankle all right?"

"I'm sure it is. I've been looking over the plot with Anna Webster, Tim's sister. It's where Tim will be buried."

"How sad, MJ. I didn't know Tim had a sister."

"I'm glad it's MJ again, Lizzie, and I'm also glad you're back. Will you be at the funeral tonight?"

"I guess so. It probably depends on what your mother and father decide I should do."

"True. I must return to Anna. Her mother is having a terrible time, and too much responsibility has fallen on Anna's shoulders. I'm trying to help, although there's not much I can do. I will see you later."

Nick returned the rest of his food to the sack. "I'm not hungry anymore, are you?" Liz shook her head. "If we're going to cross the stream, I think we'd better go. I'd like to get back before it starts to rain."

Once they crossed to the other side, Liz felt free to talk again. "Do you think Martha June heard us?"

"I doubt it. She would have said something. Come on, Lizzie—let's look around, even if I don't think we can do anything today."

Nothing looked familiar on the other side. "I think the stream must be where the narrow road separating the cemetery from the pavilion is located in the future. That came out strange, but you know what I mean." Liz was starting to confuse herself.

"I think the pavilion must have been built where that grove of trees is now." Nick shook his head. "But how are we going to use the key to get us back? It's not like we're going to find a lock. We need to stay positive, but at some point we may have to face the possibility that we aren't ever going home again."

"I know that, but I'm not ready to think about it yet."

"Let's go back to the Carpenters'. We should find out if we're expected at the funeral."

Lizzie was relieved not to see Martha June or anyone else in the cemetery when they forded the creek again.

Just as they were about to reach the Carpenters' house, Nick grabbed her and pulled her behind a tree.

"What?"

"Shhh!" he whispered. "Quiet. I want to see this."

Lizzie didn't think there was much to see. A wagon had pulled up to the store, and two men struggled to lift a large wooden crate. "Dry Goods" were the words printed on the box. Nick knew there was going to be a delivery, so what was bothering him? Mr. Carpenter came out of the store, looked both ways as if he didn't want to be seen, and gestured for the men to bring the box inside.

"Nick, what's wrong?"

"Shhh!" He led her away from the house, down the street to a patch of woods, pulling her once again behind a tree.

"Nick, you're scaring me."

"Sorry. I didn't mean to. We're not in any danger, but I don't think we were supposed to see what we just did."

"Some freight being delivered? Mr. Carpenter told you about that."

"Yes, and I also told you I didn't think he wanted me around when it happened. Don't you see, Lizzie?" She shook her head. "I remembered something I read once—maybe in Social Studies. Back in Civil War days, there were lots of codes."

"Right. Like the codes we embroidered onto the quilts."

"There were other codes, too. Like packages and freight and dry goods. Sometimes people were packed into boxes and delivered to safe houses."

"You think there's a runaway slave in that box?"

Nick nodded. "That's exactly what I think. And there were more boxes in the wagon."

"Then what, Nick? We'd know if there were runaways in the house. The only one we ever saw was Maudie."

"True, but you were sent away to the Fauls' farm, remember? And the reason I could go out there was because they didn't want me working in the store during those times."

"I guess that means Mr. Carpenter trusts Martha June after all. But why didn't they have me remain at the farm? And where are they going to hide the people?"

"Lizzie, I don't know anything for sure. I'm just guessing. As soon as I can, though, I'm going to search around the store. There must be a secret hiding place. Probably just some sort of room, but maybe a secret tunnel that leads to another safe house."

"If there is, and if you find it, then what?"

"Nothing. I'd just like to know. Maybe we'll be able to use it if we must leave quickly."

Liz thought it over. She doubted if he would succeed, but whatever they could learn was probably a good thing. "I wonder why Maudie was at the Carpenters' and not sent through a tunnel, if there is one."

"Maybe because she's so young."

"Maybe. But maybe because of her father. Mr. Faul told me he's a conductor in the URR. That's an important job, and people are very worried about him. I suppose Maudie could have used the tunnel when she left here. That was a day I missed, and I don't really know how she got to the farm. Nick, I hope you do find a tunnel. That would be so exciting!"

Chapter Fourteen

LIZ AND NICK USED THE BACK door into the kitchen, where they found Martha June all alone preparing supper. "Oh, good, I wondered what was keeping you two. Cook is ill, Lizzie, and we must hurry."

"Shall I set the table or fix the salad?" Liz noticed the salad fixings.

"The salad, please."

"I'll help," Nick offered.

"You?" MJ was clearly not used to male help in the kitchen.

"Why not? I can set a table as good as any girl. I'll put cold meat on a platter and slice up some bread. We'll keep it simple. Protein, veggie, and a carb. Not much more to do than that, is there?"

In wonder and confusion, Martha June, picking up the tray of plates and silverware, hurried to the dining room, leaving Nick and Liz to grin at each other. Seeing MJ so flustered was kind of fun, but Lizzie was relieved. It appeared there was no problem between them.

In short order, supper was ready, and Nick rang the bell. A somewhat rested Mrs. Carpenter and a satisfied looking Mr. Carpenter joined them. "It must feel strange here after the hustle and bustle at the Fauls' farm, Elizabeth."

"Just quieter, Mr. Carpenter. I had a good time there, but this is nice, too."

"Mama, Papa, Lizzie wonders if she should go to the funeral tonight."

"That is really up to Elizabeth, Martha June," her mother said. "After all, she didn't even know the boy."

That was true. Lizzie had a choice. What did she want to do? "Will you go, Nick?"

"Yes, I think I should. I knew Tim slightly and was a member of the search party. Even though it wasn't pleasant, I was their guest for one night and met the rest of the family."

Mr. Carpenter smiled. "That is good of you, Nick, considering they didn't treat you very well."

In other words, if I stay here, I'll be alone, Liz thought. "I'll come. It's the polite thing to do." All alone when there might be runaway slaves escaping through secret tunnels with evil people after them? No way!

Upstairs, Martha June helped Lizzie find a suitable frock. "You've changed your hairdo," she said. "Leah must have put you up to it."

"Yes, a chignon. She said that's what all the girls are doing."

"Your old way was more becoming, but I can see that this is easier to manage."

"I was having a hard time keeping the curls neat without help."

From her closet, MJ picked out a simple black dress and hat. "I don't suppose you can wear a bonnet with your new hair style, but this hat might do."

The hat and the dress were just plain ugly. She must have made a face because MJ started to laugh. "I quite agree," she said, "but that's all I've got. Do you want to change your mind about going?"

Liz shook her head. "No, I'll wear them." With Martha June's help, she was ready in no time. "Martha June . . . I mean MJ, are we all right? I mean you and me. About, you know, Maudie?"

MJ gave her a quick hug. "I've grown up a lot since then, Lizzie. I'm working as a teacher now, and when Eugene returns, I shall be married. I can't be a silly schoolgirl any longer. You did the right thing when you thought Maudie was in danger."

"I did think that, but now I don't know if she really was. But I'm glad we're friends again."

"We never stopped," MJ said.

The Congregational Church was filling quickly when Mr. Carpenter parked his buggy and tied his horse to a post. "Go inside and save me a seat," he told his wife. "I see someone I need to speak to." He went so quickly into the crowd, Liz couldn't tell whom he intended to see.

Right before the minister called on the congregation to rise, the Websters entered from a private door behind the pulpit and sat in a front pew. Mrs. Webster and Anna were crying softly into their handkerchiefs and Mr. Webster, with his beet red face and erratic movements, was obviously drunk.

The service was short and simple. It was also a pack of lies, Liz decided. According to the minister, Tim was a fine young man, overtaken by a dreadful accident preventing him from living on to do noble deeds for his family, town, and country. His family was upstanding, a credit to a community that must reach out and support them in their time of sorrow.

Nick probably felt the same way she did. But what else could the poor minister say? That Tim ran away from home, either because he couldn't stand it anymore or because he wanted to report that his neighbors were harboring slaves and running a station in the URR? Should he mention that Tim had no shoes and that his clothes were rags? That his father was drunk all the time and his poor mother and sister couldn't count on him for anything? No, the lies were better, but she hoped they would end soon. She hadn't wanted to be left alone but didn't want to be here either.

Finally, to the congregation's relief, came the closing prayer. Mrs. Webster and Anna left through the pastor's study, but an angry Mr. Webster stood and faced all of them. He shook his fist. "You'll pay for this," he raged. "And some of you will pay more than others." He stared angrily at the Carpenter family, especially Mr. Carpenter.

"Now, now, Jeb," the pastor said gently, leading him away. "You are going to need your neighbors. It will not do to alienate them."

"Well, that was pretty awful," Liz whispered to Nick while they waited for the others in the visiting area of the church.

"The whole thing or the ending?"

"Both, but mainly the ending. Mr. Webster gave me the creeps, and he was looking right at us."

"I agree. Makes you wonder what he meant by it. I thought the service was okay. The minister had to at least try to comfort Tim's mother and sister."

"By lying. I know. What else could he do? Oh, here they come."

Mr. Carpenter strode over to them and handed Nick a lantern. "Nicholas, I want you to escort Martha June and Elizabeth home. It's a long walk, but the evening is pleasant. You won't have any problem. Mrs. Carpenter and I will represent the family at the graveside. If there is any more unpleasantness, I don't want the girls there." Martha June opened her mouth, perhaps to protest, but stopped at her father's stern look."

"Oh, yes, Elizabeth, you'll be pleased that Leah Faul will go with you and stay the night." Liz hadn't noticed the Fauls in the crowd before but now saw an eager Leah coming toward her. "You girls mustn't stay up too late talking. Leah's father will arrive very early in the morning to pick up a delivery, and she must be ready to leave. Neither of us will have time to transport her home later in the day."

Liz and Nick looked at each other. Pick up a delivery? And what might that be, exactly?

Leah was as excited as Liz had ever seen her. "I have really missed you, Lizzie. All of us have. Ella has done nothing but whine since you left."

Considering they had been apart only a few hours, Liz found this kind of funny, but she agreed. "I've missed you, too."

"I'm glad to see you again, Leah," Martha June said. "I'm hoping you'll be able to return to school soon."

"I want to. It depends on how I feel and if Papa can take me."

Liz, who understood the seriousness of Leah's condition, quickly said, "Your health is just as important as school work." In Leah's case, it was much more important. Then, to change the subject, "How can they have Tim's burial at night? They won't be able to see."

"Lanterns," Martha June explained. "It's quite a moving sight. But actually, it will just be a graveside service. There will be a private burial tomorrow morning."

"Poor Tim," Leah said. "I wish we had tried harder to help him."

Nick nodded. "That's how I feel. Well, as the designated gentleman, I must do my duty and escort you fine young ladies home."

In spite of the circumstances, the three girls giggled and exchanged confidences all the way back while Nick pretended not to hear. As they approached, though, he held out his arm. "Wait!" he commanded. They saw what he did—a light moving about in the darkened store.

"Wait here," he said.

"Forget it," Liz said. "Strength in numbers. Whoever is in there shouldn't be, and you could be headed into danger. We go together."

"All right, but cautiously."

Lantern ready, Nick moved forward. He would have preferred handling the situation in daylight. They crept onto the porch, and then Nick threw the door wide open, startling a strange man whose lantern fell with a crash. Liz zoomed in to kick it out of the way and to extinguish the flame before it could start a fire.

Nick grabbed the man, who was shorter than he. There didn't seem to be anyone else in the room, but he ordered the girls to make sure.

"Settle down, young fellow," the man said. "I just needed to buy some goods."

"In a darkened shop with no one about—I doubt that," Martha June said, taking charge. "This is my family's store, and it looks very much as if you were planning to rob it. I don't know where you come from, but we don't take kindly to thieves around here."

"Not a thief. Was going to leave money." The man pulled some coins from his pocket."

"The store is closed, but if you're that desperate, tell me what you wished to buy, and turn over the money." Nick held out his hand, releasing the man, who took the opportunity to bolt.

Nick slammed the door. "Quickly, girls, help me push this bench over for a barricade." Martha June rushed to obey. "Now go inside and do the same with the house doors."

Leah gasped. "Nick, you let him go on purpose!"

"I did. Lizzie, help close the shutters."

Nick waited for Martha June to return before explaining. "Look, if he's a simple thief, he didn't succeed. What were we supposed to do? Sit on him until your parents came back? But if he were looking for something here—or someone—then we couldn't turn him over to the authorities. The Carpenters could be in big trouble if the police decided *they* were really the ones stealing."

Martha June nodded. "You know, don't you." It was a statement, rather than a question.

"Let's just say we figured out the store's true purpose."

"You're very smart. So is Lizzie. I only hope my foolish gossip hasn't caused problems."

"MJ, what exactly did you say to Tim?" Nick asked.

"Not much. I just said we had a colored girl staying with us for a while, and we liked her."

"That shouldn't have been a problem," Leah said.

"I don't know. No one else in town has colored help, and you should have seen the way Tim reacted."

Nick shrugged. "It's over. There's no telling how Tim interpreted what you said. It sounds harmless, but we all saw the look Mr. Webster gave us tonight. We can't take a chance."

Liz looked around the store. She couldn't see any possibilities of a hiding place. "Meanwhile, there could be someone here, hungry and afraid of being discovered."

"But safe, at least for now," MJ said.

"Maybe, but isn't there some way we can help?"

"I have an idea," Leah said. "It's a code we use sometimes." Then she began singing in her lovely low voice. *Follow the drinking gourd, follow the drinking gourd. For the old man will be waiting for to carry you to freedom if you follow the drinking gourd.*

The drinking gourd. Liz knew that code. It stood for a safe place to stop and rest. It was also called the Big Dipper and appeared on some of the quilts. She was about to compliment Leah on her singing when they heard a slight noise behind a small cupboard. Then a portion of the wall slid away, and a slender, very dark man crawled through the opening.

He smiled at them. "You young'uns don't 'pear to be old men to me," he said.

Liz grinned, guessing who he might be. "And I don't think we're strong enough to carry you to freedom either, even if we all worked together. But we are pleased to see you."

"Thankee, miss. Ah was feeling mighty cramped, but the two chillun are terrible scairt."

MJ stepped forward. "Bring them through, and I'll get them something to eat. This is my father's store. We can't guarantee your safety, but we'll surely try."

Liz, who had been examining his features, was almost certain her guess was correct. She decided to wait first to see about the other passengers on the URR. Soon, two bedraggled children—a boy and a girl in tears, came through the cabinet, and Leah rushed to comfort them. "Why, you couldn't be older than my little sister," she said. "Don't be frightened, you dear things. I'm Leah and this is Miss Martha June. She'll make certain you have something to eat and a comfortable bed. And my Papa will help you find a safer place soon."

The children responded to Leah and didn't want to part from her, so Leah accompanied them and Martha June into the kitchen, leaving Liz and Nick behind with the man.

"I think I can guess who you are," Liz said at last. "I'm almost certain you are my friend Maudie's father."

The look of joy on the man's face was overwhelming. "My Maudie? Your friend?"

"We're all her friends. She is safe but so anxious to see you, Mr . . ."

"Jes call me Samuel."

Samuel. Liz doubted that was his real name, but it didn't matter. At least she could call him something. Maudie will be—"

Nick interrupted. "Samuel, we need to decide what to do and quickly. I don't know how safe you are. We can't be certain the man who broke in was trying to steal. He might have been looking for you."

Martha June returned. "Leah is feeding the children and will bathe them. Soon they'll be cuddled up like puppies in my bed." Liz smiled. MJ *had* done some growing up.

"Thank you, Miz Martha June. Very kind."

"They're so young to be going through this. Where is their mother?"

"Far north. So will we be in a few days, God be willing."

"I hope Mr. Carpenter returns soon," Liz said. "I wouldn't think the graveside service would take long."

"Grave?" Samuel asked in alarm.

"For a local boy who had an accident," Nick said. "I do wish Mr. Carpenter could know what happened here before he gets back, though."

Martha June had brought some food for Samuel, who sat wearily on the counter stool and ate as if it were his first meal in months. "What difference would it make, Nick?" she asked.

"I don't know. Just a feeling, I guess."

Liz had been thinking. "Should one of us go to the cemetery and find him, or stop him on his way back?"

"You mean me," Nick said. "I'm not sure I should leave you alone in case the man does come back. Samuel probably should go back into the hidden room—or is it a hidden tunnel?"

The man grinned. "Laws, cap'n, wouldn't that be sumpin'? Jes a mighty small room."

Liz was disappointed. Her imagination had been captured by the idea of a secret tunnel. "You'll need three people to guard the doors, and you've got them—Nick in here, MJ in the kitchen, and Leah by the front door after she puts the children to bed. I'll go to the cemetery."

"You?" All of them protested.

"Lizzy, girls don't do things like that," Martha June exclaimed. "Although, maybe they do where you come from in Virginia . . . It does seem to be a strange place."

"Virginny?" Samuel interrupted. "Miz Lizzie is from Virginny?"

Liz stopped him fast. Anyone who knew the state and heard her speak would know she was lying. "I could borrow some of Nick's clothes and go in disguise," she said. "We're almost the same size. No one will know I'm not a boy. It will be just like a Shakespeare play in reverse."

Nick nodded. "In which men played the women parts. But I know what you mean, Lizzie. It might work. If anyone can pull it off, you can."

Martha June rose from her chair, where she had been listening almost in an amused fashion. She wasn't amused now, though; she was angry. "This is not a parlor game or a play, and you two are spouting nonsense and wasting time. Lizzie is not going to dress up as a boy and go out in the darkness to find her way to the cemetery. We appreciate your help in getting rid of the thief, or whoever he was, but the next step is a decision for grownups. Papa and Mama and Samuel have been involved in this for a long time, and it's up to them how we'll proceed. What do you think, Samuel?"

"Thankee, Miz Martha June. I'se goin' back to the hidie-hole and wait for Massa Carpenter. Jes watch over the po' chillun." And Samuel slid open the side cupboard and returned from where he had come.

Shamefaced, Liz turned to Martha June. "I'm sorry, MJ. We got carried away."

"We were just trying to help," Nick said.

"I know," she said. "Let's wait for Papa. I'm sure he'll be here soon. Lizzie, please go tell Leah to stay with the children."

They didn't have long to wait for the Carpenters' return, but a whole new shift in power had taken place. Nick and Liz were now the outsiders, as Liz was forced to admit they should have been in the first place. Their two encounters with possible slave hunters, Liz's friendship with Maudie, and, as Nick pointed out later, their arrogance in assuming that because they were from a later time they knew more, had caused them to assume roles they never should have played.

This time, they stayed quiet while Martha June explained to her parents what had occurred. Finally, Mr. Carpenter turned to Nick. "Thank you for keeping the man from exploring further," he said. "I doubt if he would have been successful, but it's good you robbed him of the opportunity to try." He turned back to his daughter.

"Martha June, you did right by aiding the children. Their fright must be unbearable. It would be safer, though, for them to be transferred to the hiding place in the closet for the remainder of the night. For now, we must all go about our business, pretending nothing is taking place here. Just before daybreak will be soon enough to proceed. Please, I'd like all of you to go into the house now. I would like to talk with Samuel in private."

They did as directed, of course. Liz and Nick would not be a part of what would happen next, nor would Mrs. Carpenter or Martha June, who were used to it being that way.

Chapter Fifteen

L IZ AWOKE WITHOUT LEAH SHARING her bed or able to tell her what day it was. She dressed quickly and scrambled downstairs for breakfast.

"You must have known Mama would say you didn't have to go to church today after staying up so late last night," Martha June said.

Oh, good. That meant today was Sunday. How long had she been here? It seemed like weeks and weeks. Could it still be October? "Where is Leah?" she asked.

Martha June laughed. "She left long ago. You must have been sound asleep. Her father came before sunrise." She rose and rinsed off her dishes. "I, for one, am going to church and need to hustle."

From her actions, it was obvious MJ had no intention of saying anything about last night's guests. Maudie and her father could be long gone by now without Liz ever saying goodbye.

Fortunately, Nick, too, decided against church. He and Liz would go for a walk. It was past time to do some serious planning.

"It's much later than we thought, Lizzie. I asked Mr. Carpenter. It's November 12."

"What happened to Halloween?"

"I have no idea, but it could have been the day of the barn dance. I finally found a calendar in the store, but usually no one remembers to flip the pages."

Liz shook her head. "It's so confusing. I can't keep track of time anymore. The real Elizabeth Gray should be here by now, and we've got to be gone before that happens."

"I agree. How is another matter. At least it's still early. Let's go to the cemetery. If we can ford the creek soon, maybe I'll be able to tell something from the sun's location."

"Good thing it's not cloudy."

"Just freezing."

So cold, in fact, that the walk was faster than usual. But the steppingstones across the creek were too slippery, causing Liz to slide off, plunging one of her boots into the water.

Nick grabbed her hand to pull her out. "Let me know if the water soaks through to your foot," he said. "We can't stay if it does. It could be dangerous."

"I'll be okay." But she could hardly control her chattering teeth. "Don't worry about me, Nick. Check the sun."

"Well, okay." He walked around, all the while gazing at the sun in the East. "Right here, Lizzie. I think this was the place."

She joined him in the middle of a circle of four trees. "Now what? Obviously, we won't find a lock."

"I don't know," he said. "It's not like the key fit the lock in the first place. Maybe once we're ready, you should just take the key and walk around the circle, holding it against the trees or even plain air."

"Shall we try now?" Liz wasn't sure she wanted to.

"Maybe, but I don't think we're done here, do you?"

Liz shook her head. "No, it feels unfinished."

"Now, at least, we have an idea of where to start the search. Let's go back so you can take off that wet boot."

By the time they reached the Carpenters, Liz was shivering all over. Mrs. Carpenter, home from church, took one look at her and hustled her into bed, where she inserted a heating iron. "Whatever were you thinking?" she exclaimed, when Lizzie told her she had slipped into the creek.

The next morning for Lizzie and Nick, unfortunately a Tuesday instead of a Monday, found Lizzie with a bad cold and forced to spend the rest of the week in bed. By Friday, she felt better—although she couldn't account for all the days in between—and rejoined the family. In private, Nick told her she hadn't missed much. He had spent time in the store and post office and had walked to the cemetery several times.

The only news of note was that Mr. Webster had left the area, and the general opinion was that he was gone for good. Mrs. Webster planned to sell the farm and move back east with her parents. Anna would remain and marry a soldier, who had returned with an injury too grave to allow him to return to battle.

"So we may never know if Mr. Webster knew anything about this being a URR station," she said.

"Or if the men we stopped were more than thieves. I doubt if Webster can do any harm, though. In his condition, he'll probably fall down and die in a ditch somewhere. Normally, I'd feel sorry for him, but because of Tim, I just can't."

Liz agreed.

Later, to her joy, Mrs. Carpenter told her she had been invited to spend the weekend with Leah. "Mr. Faul will come for you this evening after he picks her up at the schoolhouse."

"Oh, I'm glad she was able to go back," Liz said. "She likes both of her new teachers very much."

Mrs. Carpenter smiled, knowing the compliment was meant for Martha June. "We're wondering if perhaps Leah could board with us during the week this winter, enabling her to continue her schooling on a more regular basis."

"That would be wonderful," Liz said. Although nothing would keep Leah alive past the age of eighteen, perhaps the time she had left would be healthier.

"Something else will please you. The real reason you're going is to say goodbye to someone. That someone rather insisted upon it."

She means Maudie, Liz thought. "Thank you," she whispered.

At the farm, Liz was treated as if she had never left. She was given chores to do, and Mr. Faul insisted she bake another loaf of cornbread. "Yours ist best," he said, giving her a wink. While Lizzie had been away, Ella's birthday had come. She demanded that Lizzie hug the new ragdoll—a doll made to be loved and played with.

Best of all was the reunion with Maudie and her father. For the most part, Samuel hid in a special hidden section in the barn, but Maudie and Liz sneaked out to visit him whenever possible.

"Tomorrow night, we follow the North Star. Maudie be in her Mamma's arms soon." Exactly where they were going, Samuel didn't say, and Liz knew better than to ask.

"I'll never see either of you again," she said quietly. "I hope you'll be able to get word to us that you're safe."

"I'll try," Samuel promised.

Liz learned that the young children she had seen briefly when they came out of the hidden cupboard had resumed their journey on the URR with Bessie and Ivy. Samuel told her that if all went well, they would reach Canada in a few weeks.

The final parting came swiftly. "It's time," Catherine whispered after their Sunday night supper. "Go to the barn. They must leave soon."

Liz said her second goodbye to Maudie, knowing it would definitely be the last. She and Maudie embraced, but there wasn't much to be said. "I'll remember you, Maudie. Always."

"Always, Lizzie."

"Be safe."

"You be safe, too."

Liz vowed that someday she'd try to learn what happened to Maudie. Maybe she could find something in one of the history books at the library. Then she turned to Samuel. "Goodbye, Samuel. I'm glad I had a chance to meet you."

He took her hands in his and looked into her eyes. "I don't know where you come from, Miz Lizzy. Not Virginny or any other place I can tell. You know things you shouldn't, and them are things you don't know that you should." He stopped her before she could respond. "Dasn't matter. You'se a blessing, and Lord I thank thee for bringing you to my Maudie."

Then, to Samuel's certain surprise and even hers, Liz threw her arms around him and began to sob. "I wish my father was like you."

"I'se sure he's a fine man," Samuel said. He patted her on the head, "and he sure must be proud of his daughter."

Then quietly, carefully, Samuel and Maudie got into the back of the wagon, and Mr. Faul covered them first with a tarp and then with many harmless-looking products.

Liz returned to the house and smiled through her tears. She touched her locket and wished hard. Suddenly, she missed Danni.

Leah tried to cheer her. "Lizzie, here is the plan. Papa will take us into town tomorrow, so I can go to school and you can go to the Carpenters'. But won't you come to school, too, please? It's a very nice place now, and you haven't met Mrs. Oldfield or seen what a good teacher Martha June is. If you come, we'll be together a little longer."

Oh, why not? It wasn't as if she had anything else to do. She could only hope that tomorrow, for her, would be Monday. She hadn't spoken to Nick since Friday, but she imagined that if anything had changed, he would have been in touch.

Chapter Sixteen

SCHOOL HAD BECOME A HAPPIER PLACE, although Liz still found lessons from McGuffey Readers boring and the daily Bible verses troubling. Spelling bees were enjoyable, and she had no problem winning again. By recess, she had come to a conclusion. If, as Nick feared, they never returned, this life would become her reality. It was time to adjust—to accept. Here, they thought she was only twelve—too young to end her education. Keeping this in mind, Liz joined the gang in playing Snap-the-Whip and Ante, Ante, Over the Shanty. That game was kind of crazy but fun. An ordinary ball became the *ante*, and the school was the *shanty*. Someone was selected to throw the ante over the shanty, and the first person to find it was next to throw it. There was much laughter and rowdiness in their efforts, and Liz couldn't help giggling when she imagined introducing the game back at her middle school. Not that they ever had recess there; she hadn't had one since sixth grade. Here, they sometimes had it three times a day.

Games might be a hit in Drama Club, though. That was a thought to share with Mrs. Lester—if they ever returned. Liz couldn't stop hoping completely. In next year's preparations for Living Cemetery, perhaps the group could play some games and participate in other activities of the era. Ante and shanty probably wouldn't work. The school was too high and the ante would end up on the roof. She'd be in high school then, but she could go back and help . . . that is, if she ever made it home. All at once she missed it so much it seemed imperative to try again.

Mrs. Oldfield and MJ (Miss Carpenter in school, of course) came outside at the end of recess and joined the students in a relay race—something Mr. Richards never would have dreamed of doing. Leah was right, Liz thought. This assistant teaching position was exactly what MJ needed. She had joined the adult world, both here and at home. Liz could now picture her as someone's wife.

School would last until almost 5:00—dark when the students were dismissed. Not much longer now until Mr. Faul would be outside waiting for Leah and his other children. Suddenly, Liz noticed that someone else was waiting—Nick, peering through the window, anxiously trying to get her attention. How long had he been there?

MJ must have noticed, also, for she stepped outside. Liz could see Nick talking to her before rushing off. When MJ returned, she went directly to Liz and whispered, "Nick said to go to your meeting place as soon as school ends. He said you would understand." Then she went over to Mrs. Oldfield and whispered something to her, too, before grabbing her cloak and leaving the building.

What was happening? Nick must mean the tree, but they were to meet there only in an emergency. Had Maudie and Samuel been captured? But wouldn't Nick have told Martha June, and wouldn't Martha June have told Liz? Maybe not, now that she seemed to be helping her father with the URR. There was nothing Liz could do until Mrs. Oldfield finally dismissed them. Leah offered Liz a ride home, but Liz gave her a quick hug. "Not today, Leah. I'll explain tomorrow." If she was able to, that is.

Soon, the moon was bright enough to light the way, but still, Liz found the going rough. She had never walked to the cemetery alone before—and never from school. She stumbled several times, dirtying her school frock. She remembered when she had first arrived and Leah had managed to frighten her to death with her tales of timber wolves. They existed, of course. Liz had heard some at night when she was staying at the Fauls' farm. But surely there weren't any wolves this close to town. She imagined them leering at her and even thought she might have heard little barks and howls. Definitely her imagination out of control. Most certainly, if there were any beings to be frightened of, they were human. Especially a human named Lizzie Gray/Liz Havelka, she thought, trying to laugh at herself.

Once she reached the cemetery, seeing where she was going was even harder. It was much darker now, and there were too many trees. The moon, a helper before, didn't provide much light here. The trees, benign only a few mornings ago, were ghost-like and menacing. After all, this was a cemetery— the place where ghosts belonged. Were there such things? Maybe. Liz seemed to feel them lurking all around.

The cemetery was a small place. Surely she could find her oak tree. "Nicky," she stage-whispered. "Nicky, are you here?"

"Lizzie? Follow my voice. You're getting closer. I've got a lantern. Look for the light. I'll move it around until you spot it."

Finally, seeing a firefly that must be a lantern, Liz stumbled in its direction.

"Lizzie, you made it." He looked at her carefully. Her hair was disheveled, her dress a weedy, dirty mess. "I should have waited at school for you, but I thought it might help if I looked around here before you came. I'm sorry."

"I'm okay, Nick. Just tell me what happened. Is it Maudie?"

Nick shook his head. "No, it's you. Both Mr. Carpenter and I were in the post office when a message came over the telegraph machine saying that Elizabeth Gray would arrive by train in the morning and that the stagecoach would bring her here about noon tomorrow."

"Oh, no! But at least she's safe. I was worried about her."

"Better that you worry about yourself. Mr. Carpenter thinks you must be a Southern spy. I sort of talked him out of that. Reminded him of how you helped Maudie and everything. Of course, I had to pretend not to know anything for sure. I ran over to the school as soon as I could."

"We can't go back, so what do we do?"

"We cross the creek, you take off your key, and we pray."

Fording the creek at night would not be easy, but they had no other choice. Liz slipped the chain off her neck and held up the key, as if hoping it could give her the answer. "Very well, let's go."

"Put your chain back on. You don't want to drop it in the creek." But before she had a chance, Nick whispered, "What's that? Someone is coming."

A steady light came hurriedly and directly toward them. There was no use running. They must cross the creek slowly and cautiously. Whoever it was would catch up to them. They might as well see who was behind the lantern.

"Thank goodness I got here in time," the voice next to the light said.

"Martha June," Liz cried. "What are you doing here?"

"Helping you, I think. And, please, let me be MJ for a while longer. I was eavesdropping deliberately the day you said you would meet here if there were ever an emergency. It seemed so strange that the two of you were together."

"So at school, after you told me what Nick said . . ."

"I let Mrs. Oldfield know I had to go home because of an urgent family matter. Papa told me about the real Elizabeth Gray. I searched your room, Lizzie, and found this." She held out the bag that had been hidden in the closet ever since Maudie had put it there that first night. "Won't you want it wherever you're going?"

"Thank you, Martha June," Nick said. "Yes, we will need it."

Martha June held up a piece of paper. "You'll want this, too, but I did read it. It was in the cloak pocket, Lizzie. Your name is on it. I guess it really is Elizabeth, although your last name isn't Gray."

Lizzie nodded. It was the sheet from the historical society, giving her the information about Martha June's mother and her whole family. "I guess I should try to explain."

"I don't think you can. I've always known something was strange about you—that you're out of place here and need to return from wherever you came. This says my Uncle Walter is going to be killed in Tennessee. Is that true?"

"Yes," Nick said. "Very soon."

"But Eugene Farrar will return, MJ. You will be married and have a fine life with him."

"I read that, too, Lizzie, and that is good news. I don't know what else to say, other than I wish you both luck and believe that you should go quickly."

"Thank you, MJ." Liz unclasped the chain and removed the golden locket. "Don't open it until you get home. Inside are photographs of my friend, Dannisha, and me. It might confuse you even more, but I want you to have it. Then she pulled MJ into an embrace. "I will miss you, MJ. You turned out to be the best friend of all." As Liz let go, though, the key she carried in her right hand hit the trunk of the immense oak tree, and . . .

She and Nick walked out of the pavilion, in full costume, ready to take their part in the Living Cemetery.

"Oh, there you are. Hurry up! We wondered what had happened to you!"

"Danni, it's you!"

"Of course it's me, you nut! Who else would it be?"

Chapter Seventeen

NICK HAD BEEN WRONG, LIZ thought, as she entered the cemetery. The whole time her tree had been the lock, the door, their entryway back to the present. How fitting and wonderful a role for the tree she had loved.

Before taking her place in front of Martha Blanchard Carpenter's grave, Liz returned the key to Mrs. Lester, who was standing next to the information desk talking to members of the historical society.

Noticing Liz, the teacher smiled. "Good, you're ready, and you look just fine."

Liz took the key still on its chain and handed it to her. "Mrs. Lester," she said seriously, "keep the chain, and be very careful with the key. Be sure to keep it safe." She folded Mrs. Lester's fingers over it.

Mrs. Lester nodded, looking somewhat surprised, although she was used to her students being overly dramatic. "All right, dear, I will. Now, go take your place."

It wasn't long before there were more crowds around Liz and Nick than any of the other actors. Mrs. Lester opened her mouth in amazement when she realized Liz was talking about many things not included on her information sheet. And each time a group gathered around Liz and Nick, it heard slightly different stories—not just rehearsed monologues.

"My name is Martha Blanchard Carpenter," Liz said with assurance. "Although I was born in New England, my most meaningful years have taken place right here in Downers Grove with my dear husband, Henry Carpenter. Downers Grove has been good to us, in spite of the many tragedies we've experienced. And they have been considerable. Two of our sons died early— our little boy William when he was only five, and later Walter, who died in a tragic explosion. Our other Walter, my brother, was killed in the terrible war. My greatest joy, of course, has been my daughter Martha June. We were especially proud when she assisted the schoolteacher and also helped her father when our store was used as a station in the Underground Railroad. But we did decide Martha June was becoming a little too modern when she started calling herself MJ. She snapped out of that when she married Eugene Farrar."

Liz grinned inwardly at Mrs. Lester's startled expression. You didn't know those last few things, did you? You didn't know that the store was a URR station or that Martha June was a teacher and had a nickname. Those things weren't on the information sheet.

Liz was becoming chilly, wearing the purple cotton dress and the lightweight navy cloak. For warmth, she put her hands into her pockets and felt something hard. A coin? How did that get there? Liz couldn't remember putting money into the pocket. Perhaps another actor had used it in a play and forgot it. She held it up to the light. No, it was meant for her. A souvenir from the past—one of those early anti-slavery tokens—the one that said, "Am I not a Woman and a Sister?" She had seen the coins in Mr. Carpenter's store, but she hadn't touched her costume since Maudie had put it into the closet. Later, Maudie had added Nick's. In fact, Maudie and Martha June were the only ones who had ever seen the clothes. Liz smiled. She would think of it as a present from both of them, and if she ever doubted what had happened, this would speak the truth. It was impossible. It couldn't have happened. And yet it did—to her and Nick.

Almost as if he had heard her thoughts, Nick joined her. She showed him the coin. "This was in the cloak pocket."

He examined it, and then reached into his own pocket. "I've got one, too." Nick's coin portrayed a man in chains. "MJ must have put it there."

Thinking it over, Liz realized that Nick was right. Maudie wouldn't have owned the coins. She had had nothing except for the clothes on her back and her Bible. MJ had wanted Lizzie and Nick to remember her, too. Her eyes welled up, and she shivered.

"Lizzie, you're freezing. So am I. Come on—we deserve a break. The historical society is treating to hot chocolate and donuts. Let's get some." Nick shook his head. "I'm not sure whether or not to call it breakfast or supper. Lunch is a different matter. Once this is over, everyone is going across the street to Subway. Do you want to join them?"

Liz shook her head. "I think I'll head home and see if my mom is feeling better. Maybe I can help her."

"I'd like to see my family, too. They won't have missed me, of course, but . . ." Liz nodded. "But," he continued with a grin, "they won't need too much of my time. Just think—we don't have to wonder if tomorrow will be Sunday. It will be. Then we'll back at school Monday morning, as if nothing ever happened. And next weekend is Halloween. Will you go with me to the dance next Friday night?"

After all the plotting and scheming, it had become a simple question, although how they had reached this point was not so simple. "I'd love to," she said.

"But maybe skip the pink hair. Okay?"

"Okay. I think I'll be tired of it before Monday. It doesn't seem to suit me anymore. How about black with orange stripes?" Liz was flirting now, and it felt familiar and comfortable.

"As long as it's not sausage curls or a French chignon." Laughing, they reached the table and helped themselves to refreshments. Then they looked at the various displays of historical books and photos. While sipping his hot drink, Nick thumbed idly through the anniversary history book. "Lizzie, look!"

There, in front of a schoolhouse certainly built later than 1863, was a group photo of the Carpenters, the Fauls, and other townspeople—some they remembered. And standing next to Leah was a girl Liz certainly recognized—herself! "Nick, I never was in any photo, and that building wasn't built back then. But that girl is me!" They read the listing of names underneath the photo, and there it was. "Leah Faul, Elizabeth Gray, Ella Faul, Lewis Faul . . . The real Elizabeth, standing between Leah and Ella, wore a dress Liz knew well. It was her boring blue school dress, although it appeared black and white in the photo.

"This can't be me, Nick. I wasn't there."

"If you didn't have your picture taken, it can only mean that when the real Elizabeth Gray arrived, she looked exactly like you. I wonder what people made of that, or if she simply took your place as if you'd never left or never had been."

"But what did people think happened to Nicholas Arnold? Did he just disappear without anyone remembering he was there? The whole thing isn't logical, Nick."

"Logic doesn't seem to have anything to do with what happened, Lizzie."

She examined the photo more closely. This time, she studied Martha June Carpenter Farrar, standing proudly next to her husband Eugene. No one in the photo was smiling because that wasn't the fashion back then, but Liz thought MJ looked happy. She certainly was heavier. Why, she was pregnant! MJ was expecting a baby. How exciting for her! Then Liz noticed what MJ was wearing around her neck. She could just make out the tiny locket hanging on a narrow ribbon. It seemed that at least one person back then had remembered Lizzie Havelka. She would have to confess to losing Danni's gift. Hopefully, she wouldn't be upset, especially since Liz would buy new ones for each of them. If only she could explain what had happened, but no one—not even Danni—would believe her. Even if Nick backed her, everyone would think both were crazy. The truth belonged only to her and Nick and, perhaps, the next Drama Club member who came late to the Living Cemetery and used the magic key.

"Liz, Nicky, come and see!" Danni was calling them.

She and the other Drama Club members were gathered around an open area quite close to the road—a place absent of any gravestones. "You want to see something weird?" Danni asked, once they joined the group. "I'm sure this wasn't here a few minutes ago. It just appeared—almost like magic. Spooky!"

Liz followed Danni's finger, pointing to a perfect circle of mushrooms, an almost fairy-like ring, large enough to surround a giant oak tree—if there had been one.

Nick took Liz's hand and squeezed tightly. "Only one explanation," he whispered. "The ghosts of the cemetery did it. It is the ghost of a tree remembered."

Late October 2016

"MRS. LESTER, HI! BET YOU thought we wouldn't come."

"Liz, Nick—oh, this is fine. I wasn't sure now that you're in college." Mrs. Lester turned and introduced them to Miss Porter. "These are my two most loyal former students, Liz Havelka and Nick Aubrey. Liz and Nick, Miss Porter will be taking over Drama Club soon."

The three murmured hellos. Then Liz gave Mrs. Lester a quick hug, hoping to conceal tears that had begun to form. She could tell Miss Porter noticed, though. "Of course we came. We've never missed a year of Living Cemetery, not since we almost missed it when we were in eighth grade."

"No, you haven't." Mrs. Lester smiled in delight. "But now that you're in college, I certainly couldn't expect it."

"We came home late last night and return tomorrow afternoon," Nick explained. "Liz is staying at my house since . . ."

"Yes, I read that your mother passed away. I'm so sorry, dear."

"Thanks. It was hard." Liz paused. "My, it's good to be back, although everything looks so much smaller."

"A big university can do that," Miss Porter said, joining the conversation. "That is, if you're going to one."

Nick nodded. "Pretty big. The U of I at Champaign-Urbana."

Mrs. Lester sighed. "But neither is majoring in theater, in spite of the fabulous department there. Still science and history?"

"Yes, I'm majoring in history. I'll probably be a teacher someday, although research is what interests me most. Nick is the scientist."

"Space and time—things like that. It's all a bit uncertain."

"You don't need to decide yet," Mrs. Lester said. "You're young and healthy. And are the two of you still . . ."

Nick laughed, throwing an arm around Liz's shoulder. "Still together since our own Living Cemetery five years ago."

Liz blushed, then drew her left hand from her pocket and flashed her sparkling fourth finger.

"Oh, my . . . Or I guess I should say congratulations and best wishes."

"Don't worry," Nick assured Mrs. Lester. "We won't be married for a long, long time. You see, except for me and my family, Liz is all alone now. This kind of makes her a part of us sooner."

"I love all of them," Liz said. "It nice to still have a home here, and . . ."

"Mrs. Lester, I'm back!" Suddenly, a girl flew toward them, gray cape sweeping out behind her. "Oh, sorry, I didn't mean to interrupt, but I was so worried I wouldn't make it and . . ."

"You're just in time, Kim. Relax and catch your breath. I want you to meet a couple of our former Thespians."

"Oh, okay. But first, here's your key." Then, as Liz had done five years before, she placed the key into Mrs. Lester's hand, enclosing her fingers around it. And just as seriously as Liz had done said, "Don't ever let anything happen to it."

Finally, Kim stared at Liz and Nick. "I'm sure I've seen you before."

Liz smiled at her. "Probably right here. We come back every year."

"No, that's not it." Kim shook her head. "We just moved to Downers Grove over the summer. But I know I've seen you somewhere."

"Kim, it's time. They're coming!"

"Gotta go. Maybe we'll talk later?" Kim dashed off.

"Who is she portraying?" Liz asked.

"Leah Faul," Miss Porter said. "And I'm afraid she is woefully unprepared."

Liz and Nick looked at each other. Leah Faul. Perhaps Kim had met them.

Mrs. Lester patted her worried assistant's shoulder. "I'm sure Kim will be wonderful, Ann. No need to worry about any of these young people. Just love them."

"A little more discipline would not hurt, Claire. I'm going to see for myself how Kim is doing."

Liz turned again to her teacher for another hug. This time she didn't bother hiding the tears.

"It's all right, dear. I'll be all right."

Nick tried to lighten the mood. "But will the kids be? Miss Porter is totally different from you."

"And perhaps that will be a good thing. I have confidence in Ann Porter. Besides, the students will teach her. If you'll excuse me now, I think a trip to the ladies' room might be a good thing, too."

Arms around each other, Liz and Nick watched Mrs. Lester pass by where once grew the largest oak tree they'd ever seen, cross a narrow road that was once a branch of St. Joseph's Creek, to finally reach the pavilion. Neither was surprised when she ignored the public restrooms and approached a door seldom used. Slowly, she held up the key, examined it carefully, and then, without looking back, pressed the key next to the lock.

"You were right, Claire. Kim is absolutely marvelous. And she wasn't at all ready yesterday. Claire . . . Why, where did she go?"

"I'm not sure, Miss Porter."

Nick shook his head. "Liz and I were talking, and I'm afraid we didn't see which way she went."

Ann Porter shed her good mood. "Honestly, that kind of thing happens too often. She has become so flighty, I'm beginning to see why the school board encouraged her to retire."

Liz stared at her. "You don't know, do you?" Trying not to cry, she walked away, leaving Nick to take over.

Nick cleared his throat. "Miss Porter, I shouldn't have to be the one to tell you this, but the school board didn't ask Mrs. Lester to leave. It was her decision to resign. She's dying. She only has a few months left to live. That's the real reason Liz and I came today—to say goodbye."

"Dying? I . . . Oh, why wasn't I told? I would have been more patient."

"Maybe that's why she didn't want you to know. She just wanted you to be yourself."

"But I haven't been a very nice self," Miss Porter muttered, as if they weren't there. "Oh, where is she? I must find her."

Liz turned back. "Maybe you should wait for her to find you," she said. "You're in charge now. Why don't you go around and listen to the students? They like it when you take pictures, too. And they'll want you to go with them to Subway for lunch afterwards."

Liz and Nick watched the flustered new director hurry back to her students.

"Subway for lunch?" Nick grinned. "And maybe the Halloween dance next Friday?"

"Yes, at least some things stay the same."

Liz gazed at the pavilion. Good luck, Mrs. Lester. Do help them out on the Underground Railroad, and ask MJ to show you her locket. "Nick, do you think Mrs. Lester will start a Drama Club at the old school on Maple Avenue?"

"Sure to. That'll shake 'em up."

"Have a wonderful adventure, Mrs. Lester. I hope you'll have years and years ahead of you in your new home. Nick, let's go hear what Leah Faul might say that is not on her information sheet."

Then Nicholas Arnold and Elizabeth Gray, and Nick Aubrey and Liz Havelka walked hand in hand to the Fauls' family gravesite.

What's Real and What Isn't About
The Ghost of a Tree Remembered

EACH FALL, EARLY ON A Saturday morning shortly before Halloween, the Downers Grove Historical Society sponsors a popular event called the Living Cemetery. Herrick Middle School's Drama Club participates in this reenactment of sorts, in which they and other actors pretend to be the village founders buried in our historic Main Street Cemetery. The cemetery is a charming place that has been in existence far too long to be considered the least bit scary—even at Halloween time. It is also one of the few cemeteries in the United States located on the main street of a town.

The modern characters in this novel are fictitious but are based on theater students I've enjoyed working with through the years. The majority of the people Liz and Nick meet in the past, though, did exist, and most of the information about them is correct.

During the Civil War era, many residents of Downers Grove were abolitionists, who took part in maintaining the Underground Railroad. Some stations still remain in the village and in nearby communities, chiefly the Blodgett home, now located on the site of the Downers Grove Historical Museum, and Graue Mill, today located Oakbrook, Illinois. The Carpenters were active in the abolitionist movement, and their store was used as a meeting place to make plans for the Underground Railroad.

The Webster family and Maudie and her father are fictitious. As far as I know, Kate Dixon Oldfield was never a teacher, nor was Martha June Carpenter her assistant. I do thank them for filling in as fictional substitutes for that awful, though fictitious, Mr. Richards.

Writing *The Ghost of a Tree Remembered* became a meaningful education as I haunted the Main Street Cemetery, the Downers Grove Museum, library, and Graue Mill, digging for more information about the brave people who were instrumental in making our village of Downers Grove the outstanding community it is today.

About the Author

THE GHOST OF A TREE REMEMBERED is Marilyn Ludwig's seventh book. She lives in Downers Grove, Illinois, where she is a theater director at Herrick Middle School. She is a member of the Downers Grove Historical Society and the Society of Children's Book Writers and Illustrators (SCBWI).

www.ingramcontent.com/pod-product-compliance
Lightning Source LLC
Chambersburg PA
CBHW020620120726

47905CB00003B/877